INNOCENCE
DENIED

INNOCENCE DENIED

*A Desperate Unbeliever is Blessed
with Divine Intervention*

Mike Garrett

CrossLink Publishing

CrossLink Publishing
558 E. Castle Pines Pkwy, Ste B4117
Castle Rock, CO 80108
www.crosslinkpublishing.com

Ordering Information:
Quantity sales. Special discounts are available on quantity purchases by corporations, associations, and others. For details, contact the "Special Sales Department" at the address above.

Innocence Denied/Garrett —1st ed.

ISBN 978-1-63357-146-4

Library of Congress Control Number: 2018941445

First editon: 10 9 8 7 6 5 4 3 2 1

CHAPTER ONE

Talladega County, Alabama

A cool, gentle breeze blew whitecaps across Logan Martin Lake's beautiful 275-mile shoreline. Leaves shimmied overhead in trees that lined Kradle Kove, and fallen pine needles skittered across the lawn in the wind. In the distance a Jet Ski buzzed across sparkling blue water. Overhead came the steady drone of an airplane, obscured by hardwoods and pines surrounding the house.

Fifty-four-year-old Derrick Walton stepped outside onto the deck of his lake house overlooking the water and slid the glass door shut behind him, the sound of Credence Clearwater Revival blasting from the stereo inside. He set a glass of iced tea on the picnic table in front of his older sister, Karen Danvers, then dropped into an adjacent chair as he sipped a glass of his own.

"Derrick, it's not like you to be this withdrawn," she said, a look of concern etched across her face. "You're losing too much weight, and you're not yourself anymore," she continued. "This is an awful time for you to go gallivanting across the country away from me. I'm all you've got left."

Derrick swept a hand across his receding hairline and sighed. Still slightly overweight despite having recently lost several pounds, his belly strained against the waistline of his pants, and the undersized long-sleeve T-shirt he wore stretched tightly against his chest as he inhaled. He hadn't shaved in days.

For the first time ever he noticed the aging in Karen's face and her predominantly gray hair. The two were indeed getting older. Where had the time gone? It seemed like only yesterday he had pestered her as a child, hiding her favorite doll, Betsy, and making her cry.

Suddenly he felt a nudge on his shoulder. "Derrick! Are you listening to me?" Karen said in an irritated tone.

Jarred back to reality, he answered, "I'm sorry, Sis. Guess I got a little preoccupied."

"So what's your answer? Why now, and why so far away?"

Derrick took a deep breath and exhaled. "It's just something I have to do. I don't expect you to understand."

He noticed more worry in her voice than he'd heard before, even when times seemed at their worst. "Scooter, I know you still miss Sherry, bless your heart, but you need me now instead of just running away."

"I'm not running from anything," he snapped, then apologized. "Sorry. You know I've been through a lot lately, and I just need to get away for a while, that's all."

Karen projected a weak smile, lightly shaking her head. "I still can't believe she said those awful things to you before she . . . It makes me madder than a wet hen. You didn't deserve—"

"I'm not so sure about that," he interrupted. "If I was such a great husband, why didn't I see it coming? If I was as attentive as I should have been, I would have noticed the changes in her. She lost weight and was getting back into shape and changing her hairstyle. I was stupid enough to think she was doing it for me. If I hadn't been so blind, she never would have had a reason to look elsewhere."

He buried his face in his hands and stifled a tear, hating the way his emotions overwhelmed him at times like this. After all he'd been through, at this point he expected to be stronger.

"But why do you have to go now, of all times, so far away? Couldn't you just go some place closer to home like Gulf Shores or Little River Canyon for a few days?"

"I told you already, I happened to find a short-term lease on a cabin in Cottonwood, and I'm familiar with the area."

"Oh Derrick." He heard her sigh in frustration. "I thought you were done with Arizona. And it'll dredge up old memories for sure."

"Not as many memories as there are around here. Sherry and I only lived in Arizona two years, and that was what, five or six years ago? Besides, it's the perfect place to clear my head without any distractions and get my life back on track."

Dixie, a black Labrador retriever mix that had recently joined his household, slowly padded up the steps behind Karen, and Derrick knew she would be surprised. Dixie's tail showed her delight in seeing her master as the dog sat beside him on the deck and raised her head to be scratched.

"And who is this?" Karen asked.

He smiled. "This is Dixie, my traveling buddy. She'll keep me company in Cottonwood."

"I didn't know you had plans to get a dog," Karen said.

"I didn't," Derrick answered, "but Dixie had plans of her own."

"Another abandoned dog, huh?"

"Yep. People should be ashamed dumping helpless animals in the middle of nowhere and expecting them to survive. It makes me furious."

"So you didn't even try to find her owner?"

"Are you kidding me? You know how many stray dogs have been dropped off around here before. And Dixie's smart. If there was any way she could get back to her owner, she would have, I promise you."

He leaned over and scratched under Dixie's neck. Her big tongue curled out and licked his hand. "I've had her a couple of weeks now, and she's just what I've needed."

The Jet Ski on the lake buzzed closer. Two teenagers aboard cheered as they created a surge of waves that rocked Derrick's floating pier. He smiled. It was heartwarming to see kids enjoying innocent fun even after the fall weather had turned cool.

"Okay, so you tried to change the subject by introducing Dixie to me, but I'm not done trying to convince you to stay," Karen said.

Derrick exhaled deeply and took another sip of tea. "Karen . . . I can design websites in Cottonwood as easily as I can here. I get all my business online, and I pay my bills electronically, too. I don't plan to stay there long; a couple of months, three or four at most."

"*Months*? Goodness, Derrick, I thought you'd only be gone a couple of weeks! Months? This is worse than I imagined."

Derrick slowly shook his head and tried not to let the pain inside show. There was so much that Karen didn't know, even though he was closer to her than anyone else on the planet. He glanced at the house he so dearly loved. To the left of the sliding door his rusted barbecue grill rested in a corner of the deck, complete with a propane tank collecting dust. A couple of potted plants that would need to be taken inside for the winter occupied the opposite corner. The front of his home was virtually all windows, and the view of the lake from inside was amazing. The opposite shore was over a mile across the water.

He would miss this place, having lived here the better part of the past sixteen years. He would miss Karen, too, but it would only be for a short while. It was hard to explain to her why he needed to leave temporarily. He wasn't even sure himself why he felt so compelled to go, but he knew that he could deal with his latest personal crisis better there than here.

The isolation in Arizona would be perfect. He'd already blocked every number on his cell phone but Karen's and unsubscribed from all the emails he could and deleted the rest. He had a lot of thinking to do without any interference.

"Sis, I'll miss you, but we can talk every day. Anyway, it's all set. I'm leaving tomorrow."

"*Tomorrow*?" Karen leaned over and gave him a tight hug. "You're hopeless. You're also the stubbornest man I've ever known. Even though you terrorized me when we were kids, I can't help but love you so."

"Me, too, Sis, and I'll get over this, I promise."

Dixie spotted a squirrel scampering across the yard. She barked and raced down the steps in a futile attempt to catch it but was too late.

"Don't worry about me. I'll be fine," Derrick said, but he felt that perhaps he was trying to convince himself more than her.

CHAPTER TWO

Flagstaff, Arizona

T ension inside the car rose steadily before they even arrived at the site of the proposed hit. Hank Spyker already seethed inside. Kenneth Baxter had insisted that they do a run-through prior to the actual murder to "be sure that you don't screw anything up."

Spyker shook his head as he quietly stared at the smug jerk in the driver's seat. He had done plenty of hits and never needed a rehearsal before. While it was true that this would be his first female, that mattered little to him, although he had to admit that the more time he spent with Baxter, the less he liked the man, and the more sympathy he felt for his wife. Maybe she'd be better off dead instead of stuck living with such an egotistical maniac. He'd seen a photo of the target; how could Baxter think he could do better than that?

More than once he'd wished that he had never connected with Baxter. He was the most arrogant scumbag he'd ever met. Spyker didn't need the money all that much, and Baxter was becoming far more trouble than he was worth.

As the late model Cadillac Escalade whisked up the winding driveway, Spyker stretched his long, lean legs out in front of him. Cough drop wrappers filled the driver's side cup holder, and a pile of miscellaneous trash lay scattered across the floor; however, the plush leather seats of this mobile dumpster were quite comfortable. Baxter gripped the steering wheel in a haughty stance. The smell of his cologne was almost stifling within the confines of the car, and his short black hair and scruffy beard were barely visible in the darkness. Who the heck wore sunglasses at night?

They approached a large basement garage boasting three doors, and as the middle door lifted, the light inside the garage came on. Once the car was parked, Baxter cut the ignition and said, "Stay here while I make sure she's asleep."

Spyker quietly nodded. *What next?*

Exiting the car to await Baxter's return, he stretched his thin six-foot-two frame, ran a hand over his short spiked red hair, and leaned against the Mercedes parked beside the Escalade. After seeing the impressive real estate and expensive cars, he knew he was being underpaid and was tempted to renegotiate the deal. Tripling what Baxter had offered for the hit would still be chump change to someone with such a seemingly hefty bank account.

Quietly returning to the garage, Baxter interrupted Spyker's thoughts, giving a thumbs up that signaled all was well upstairs. Spyker knew what was coming next. As expected, Baxter's know-it-all mouth spewed orders nonstop. "I'll show you everything outdoors. I'll take care of the details; you just get the job done."

They stepped outside the garage and around the back corner of the house toward a fence surrounding the moonlit swimming pool. Spyker hesitated to call it a "house"; it looked more like a palace to him. An owl made itself known in a nearby tree.

Spyker glanced around the back of the mansion. "Where's Pickett?" he asked.

"Forget Pickett. It's just you and me now," Baxter said. "You're probably smart enough to handle it alone."

Probably? Spyker forced a laugh and scrubbed his shoes against the smooth pebbled landscaping outside of the fence. "So if it's just me doing the whole job, I get the whole payout, right?"

Baxter sneered and shook his head in silent response.

Baxter's last comment still echoed in Spyker's mind. *Probably smart enough?* The thought made him fume inside. He tugged a pack of cigarettes from his shirt pocket, but Baxter pushed them away. "Not here," he said. Spyker seethed.

Baxter pointed to a window on the second floor directly above the pool. "That's the bedroom. She's on Ambien, so she'll be out like a light," he said. "I'll be out of town, and no one will be home but her."

Spyker wasn't concerned about waking her. That would actually make the hit more challenging, but he wanted no more distractions than that. "Any dogs?" he asked.

"No." Baxter essentially shrugged off the question and led him to an ornate back door. "I'll tell her there's a short in the alarm system and that she shouldn't set it until it's repaired. Just break the window, reach inside, and flip the deadbolt."

"Oh, yeah," Spyker said sarcastically with a roll of his eyes. "I never would've thought of that." He exhaled deeply, then asked, "What if she sets it anyway?"

Baxter slowly shook his head. "She won't. I'll check it remotely to be sure. I can disable it with my cell phone if I have to."

With an intense expression, Baxter continued, "Look, Spyker, I'm just being cautious. We've got to be on the same page every step of the way. We've both got a lot to lose."

"Yeah, sure." Spyker felt his pulse rise. If Baxter kept this up, he was sure he'd reach his breaking point.

Baxter reached into his pocket and pulled out a compact Beretta Pico .380 caliber pistol. "This is from my gun collection. When you go through that door, you'll be in the kitchen. The next room will be my study. The gun cabinet is in there, so if you want to take anything, help yourself. Make it look like a burglary and grab whatever you want. Insurance will cover it. Just be sure to wear latex gloves." He offered the handgun to Spyker. "It's loaded."

Spyker examined the gleaming semiautomatic pistol. It was lightweight and well made. He'd never used a fancy gun before, but it could definitely do the job.

Spyker cleared his throat. "So, you got some special way you want this done?"

Baxter smirked. "You don't have much of a memory, do you, Spyker? Two to the head, like I told you."

Spyker groaned, gave a low, deep laugh, then said, "Yeah, sure; I mean besides that. Anything else you want done to her? You want me to drag it out, make her suffer? You want her to know you sent me?" he asked. Spyker was big on customer service.

Baxter hesitated, glaring at the upstairs window, then said, "Yeah, tell her happy anniversary." A sinister grin spread across his face. "You can do anything you want to her as long as you make it quick. Just don't leave any evidence, if you know what I mean. The longer you're here, the more likely you are to make a mistake, and if you go down, I go down with you."

Spyker nodded. Baxter grinned. "The only difference is, I've got the money to buy the best lawyers in Phoenix, and you don't."

This guy was really pushing his buttons. Spyker's anger hadn't been provoked this much in quite some time. He simmered inside.

From another pocket Baxter took out a roll of cash bound with a rubber band. "Here's the five thousand, like I promised. There's ten more after it's done."

Spyker nodded and accepted the advance payment, soothing his temper somewhat.

"Now," Baxter said, glaring beyond the swimming pool, "the rear of the property adjoins the park where we left your car. You can easily get away without being seen."

Spyker began to pace back and forth at the edge of the pool. "Now, how far is this walk? I didn't sign up for no hike."

"No more than half a mile at most. It's not bad; you'll see when you walk back to your car tonight."

"Say what?"

"I want you to familiarize yourself with the land. No screw-ups, right?"

Spyker exhaled deeply and swallowed hard. "I ain't in the mood for no nighttime stroll in the park. There's coyotes in them woods. You can take me back to my car."

The veins in Baxter's neck and forehead bulged. He leaned into Spyker's face and, through gritted teeth, demanded, "Listen to me, you half-witted felon. You do exactly as I say or—"

"Or what? The deal is off? You'll do it yourself? You'd have to grow a pair for that."

Spyker knew that Baxter was struggling to control his rage. What Baxter didn't know, however, was that he was directing his wrath toward a killer with far more dangerous anger issues than his own, and that could prove deadly. After hurling expletives at each other like darts at a bull's-eye, Spyker finally calmed down enough to ask, "So, how many punks did you ask to do this before you got around to me? You think you're so careful about everything; how many loose ends did you leave?"

"Nobody. Just you and Pickett. If you hadn't agreed to do it, I was going to make it look like an accident," Baxter said. His eyes narrowed. "I thought you had plenty of experience. I didn't think I'd have to hold your hand to pull this off."

"Pickett's a problem. Why didn't you tell me he ditched you before tonight?"

The veins in Baxter's forehead bulged. He shoved Spyker hard toward the fence surrounding the pool area. Spyker shoved back. Baxter then stepped through the gate and paced to the edge of the pool, breathing hard, clenching his fists. A coyote howled from somewhere nearby.

Think you're a tough guy, huh? Spyker thought. He took a deep breath and felt himself losing control. Gripping the pistol, he weighed his options. It seemed more and more promising to cut his losses now, settle for just the advance payment, and be done with this whole thing.

"Forget it," Baxter said. "Give me the cash back. Now."

Spyker took three long steps through the gate to join Baxter at the pool's edge. His heart pounded, his breath grew heavy. An evil smile blanketed Spyker's face. "No, you forget it," he snapped, and with that, in one swift motion, he put the barrel of the Beretta to the back of Baxter's head and fired twice. "There's your two to the head!"

Baxter splashed facedown into the pool, a cloud of pink spreading from around his head like a crimson oil spill staining the otherwise clear water. Spyker angrily threw the gun at the lifeless floating body. It bounced off with a soft thud and tumbled into the water. Spyker raced to the other side of the pool, leaped over the fence, and continued into the darkness beyond the property that led to his car in the nearby park.

CHAPTER THREE

One week later

Cottonwood, Arizona

After unpacking what little was left in the cargo space of his Chevy Tahoe, Derrick wiped sweat from his forehead, exhausted. The three-day stopover in Taos had provided much-needed rest, but it felt good to have finally reached his destination. He scanned the front of the rental house conveniently located only an hour or so southwest of Flagstaff. The two-bedroom adobe-style home was boxlike in appearance, vastly different from the typical homes in Alabama that he was accustomed to. He rarely saw flat-roofed houses back home. The front lawn, if one could call it that, was covered in pebble-sized river rocks and cacti.

In the distance loomed Mingus Mountain and the city of Jerome. He wondered if he'd be able to hear the whistle of the trains embarking on the Verde Canyon scenic railroad in nearby Clarkdale. The depot wasn't far away. The memory of a train ride with Sherry started to form, but he quickly pushed it away.

Dixie seemed nervous, and Derrick couldn't blame her. He recalled the first time he'd ventured west on a road trip with a buddy shortly after he graduated from college. The terrain couldn't have been more different from his native Alabama, and he felt as if he'd landed on another planet that first time. Dixie would get used to it, though. She would be happy as long as she was with him.

He opened the front door and motioned Dixie inside, afraid to leave her outdoors for fear of rattlesnakes. Having stored what few things he had brought in the spare bedroom, he wondered how long he would actually stay here. Even though there hadn't been anything heavy to carry, he was still winded from the exertion of unloading the car and paused to catch his breath.

Derrick collapsed onto the sofa. Dixie hopped up to join him, laying her big black head on his lap. He scratched her back, considering how much lonelier he would be if she hadn't shown up in his yard back home. He doubted that the thought of getting a dog would have ever crossed his mind, yet now she was an integral part of his life, a perfect companion and a gift from above. There hadn't been any lack of surprises over the last couple of years.

For a moment he just stared into space and shook his head. What was he supposed to do now? When he looked back on his life, he had little to show for his years. What had he truly accomplished? How had he positively impacted the lives of others? He'd been so self-centered that he hadn't even noticed Sherry's love for him fading. He'd focused so much on his own happiness that he hadn't considered that her heart might have drifted elsewhere.

Looking forward, what could he do to make the rest of his life worthwhile? After he was dead and gone, would anyone have a positive word to say about him? At the moment he couldn't think of anything. He felt like a single ant in a mound of millions, the same as all the others, nothing outstanding about him in the least. Was that how meaningless his existence was meant to be?

Perhaps after spending some time here he would figure it out.

The next morning, after a cup of coffee, Derrick booted up his iPad to see what was going on back home. On his My Yahoo homepage, local news headlines popped up instead of his hometown news, and one item immediately caught his attention: *Accused Baxter Killer Posts Bond.* There was nothing of particular note about the story; he'd seen similar posts hundreds of times, but what stood out most was the postage stamp-sized photo that accompanied the article—a beautiful, young, dark-haired woman who looked nothing like any killer he'd ever seen. What made it even more impressive was the fact that it was a mug shot taken at the police station, which typically showed people at their worst. If this was her worst, how might she look at her best?

Derrick shook his head and sighed. I guess we all have problems, he thought. Even the beautiful people.

CHAPTER FOUR

Flagstaff, Arizona

Since Ken's death, the house had been overwhelming, its emptiness almost engulfing her. Even the housekeeper refused to return to a residence now designated as a crime scene. Larissa Baxter sat in a daze on the sofa of her massive living room trying hard to focus on the words of her defense attorney, Harvey Bateman. Her cup of Starbucks on the coffee table had long since chilled before she'd taken a single sip. She found it difficult to concentrate; her world had been turned upside down in a matter of days, and she was now in a situation she never dreamed possible.

The murder of her husband hadn't come as a complete surprise; he had plenty of enemies, through both his business dealings and personal connections, but the biggest shock of all came when she was named as a person of interest, then arrested for a crime she didn't, and would never, commit.

"Larissa, I don't think you understand," Bateman said. "This is not about the truth; it's about the prosecution's case and whether or not a jury will believe it."

Larissa groaned. "But how could the truth be so difficult to defend?" she asked.

"Well, sometimes it is," Bateman answered after taking a sip of coffee. "You've got to help me dismantle their version of the crime."

"And that is?"

Bateman cleared his throat. "That you were angry about something while Ken was away, took the Beretta from his gun cabinet, and waited for him in the garage. When he got home, the argument escalated and for some reason moved outside by the pool, where you shot him, threw the gun into the water after he fell in, then jumped in yourself to supposedly save him, but really only did so to wash the gunshot residue from yourself."

"But that's not what happ—"

"Larissa, you're not listening," he interrupted. "The Beretta came from Ken's gun cabinet, and you yourself said that no one else was in the house at the time, putting yourself at the crime scene. There was no sign of forced entry." Bateman slowly shook his head. "Again, this is not about the truth; it's about countering the prosecution's allegations."

Larissa noticed how Bateman's gaze into her eyes lingered longer than appropriate, well aware of the effect her appearance had on men. Briefly she regretted having worn such a tight outfit for this meeting, yet in hindsight, she realized that everything she owned accentuated her near-perfect figure. She rested her head against the back of the sofa and stared up at the massive light fixture suspended from the twenty-foot ceiling, then ran her hands through her long dark hair and wiped tears from her cheeks. "I've already told you, the gunshots woke me up. Well, I didn't know it was gunshots at the time; something just woke me up. I was groggy from a sleeping pill." She took a deep breath, then continued. "I looked out the bedroom window and saw him floating facedown in the pool. I thought he had fallen in and was drowning, so I ran downstairs and jumped in to save him."

"Did you ever touch the gun?"

"I didn't even know a gun was there. I saw a cloud of blood in the water, but it didn't dawn on me that he'd been shot until the police told me later. I thought he had hit his head when he fell in."

Larissa took a deep breath in an attempt to calm her nerves. It didn't work. Her expression brightened as she said, "My fingerprints won't be on the gun since I never touched it! Shouldn't that clear me?"

Bateman pursed his lips and slowly shook his head. "There were no prints at all on the gun. The water or chlorine or whatever destroyed them." After another sip of coffee he added, "Ken's fingerprints were on the ejected shell casings, which is only natural since it was his gun, and he probably kept it loaded."

Larissa's disappointment was obvious as she looked Bateman directly in the eyes and argued, "Anyway, I have my own gun. Why would I go downstairs and get one from Ken's gun cabinet when I already had one of my own?"

Bateman scribbled notes onto a yellow legal pad. "That's good. We need to make more points like that." He paused, apparently in deep thought, then asked, "How long did you wait before calling nine one one?" he asked.

"I don't know . . . only a couple of minutes. I had no reason to wait."

Bateman nodded. "Do you have any idea why the garage door was left open?"

"I didn't know it was open. This is the first I've heard of that. I went out the back door to the pool," she said.

Bateman tapped his pen against the legal pad and stroked his chin with his fingertips. "Think hard. Is there anything else?"

She wanted to remember, but truth be told, she had had a few drinks in addition to Ambien that night, and her memory was foggy at best. "I don't know what else to say," she finally responded. "It all happened so fast."

Bateman pushed his black-framed glasses up his nose and sighed. "Larissa, if you can't give me more than this, we may have no choice but to accept a plea bargain of some kind. At least that could get the death penalty off the table if that's what they're going after."

Larissa was incredulous. "How could the death penalty even be a possibility when their whole case is just speculation? The only concrete fact they have is that I was at home when it happened!"

Bateman slowly shook his head. "I've seen men convicted with far less evidence," he said.

"And women?"

"Well, being an attractive woman would be in your favor if the Baxters weren't involved. They'll pull out every skeleton from your past and paint you as an evil, vindictive woman. At some point you'll need to tell me what kind of bones they might find."

She saw that he was deeply concerned and began to realize that she should be, too. "You've got to understand," he continued, "you're going up against one of the most powerful families in northern Arizona. They're already freezing your assets and coming at you with both barrels. They're more concerned about protecting their image than justice for Ken. They want this over quickly to get themselves out of the spotlight, and they're ruthless, Larissa. They can put a lot of pressure on the district attorney."

He paused a moment and looked her square in the eyes. "Look, I'm only telling you this to prepare you for what lies ahead. It's far too early to even think about a plea deal, but from the information I have so far, that's the direction we're headed. I'm just warning you."

Wiping back a wisp of hair from her eyes, Larissa said, "Half of the people in this county wanted him dead, but the police are only looking at me."

"And that brings up the subject of motive," Bateman said as he scratched his chin. "You've got to be straight with me, Larissa. What will you gain from Ken's death?"

Larissa laughed, then her expression turned grave. "On paper, a lot," she said, "but in reality, practically nothing."

"What do you mean?"

"Well, unless he's made a change in his will, he left everything to me," she answered.

"And what do you mean by *practically nothing*?" he pressed further.

Larissa reached for her coffee cup, then pulled her hand back, remembering that it had grown too cold to drink. "Well, first of all, we were heavily in debt—much more so than anyone would imagine. After paying off everything that we owe, I doubt there will be much left."

"And second?"

She laughed again. "You said it yourself. The Baxters are ruthless, and they're greedy, too. They'll fight me tooth and nail to keep me from coming away with anything."

"Hmm," Bateman responded. "Any life insurance?"

With a shrug Larissa answered, "Of course not! Ken had no interest in protecting me financially in the event of his death. Besides, he thought life insurance was a waste of money."

Nodding after a sip of coffee, Bateman stared at her as if expecting more.

"I've known for years that I would never take anything away from this marriage if we split," she continued. "I was miserable, but I guess I stuck with him to avoid the conflict that would come with leaving him."

"That may well be the case, but I prefer that you not say things like that. What has Ken's demeanor been like lately? Has he been upset about anything or mentioned any recurrent problems?"

Larissa shrugged. "Upset? Ken had no feelings. He didn't care about anyone but himself. Jealous husbands and cheated business partners were probably standing in line to take him out, but no one in particular comes to mind."

Bateman held up his hand. "Let me stop you right there," he said. "There's a lot of bitterness toward Ken in your tone today. That won't play well with a jury. Don't talk to anyone, anywhere, like that about him. It could come back to haunt you."

CHAPTER FIVE

Cottonwood, Arizona

As Derrick ended a call with his sister, he set his cell phone beside him on the sofa, feeling guilty for lying to her again. Well, technically, he'd been more deceptive than outright dishonest. He had implied that nothing new was going on in his life—nothing that she was unaware of—and that he would still be working while in Arizona, yet he had no intention of doing so. He knew he was guilty of lying by omission for not telling her everything, but there would be a time for that later.

He had completed all of his work assignments prior to leaving Alabama and was accepting no new business. Call it early retirement or whatever, but he was done with it. This trip was all about wrapping his head around the rest of his life and what God might have in mind for him. He never wanted to be defined by his work alone anyway. He hoped the first thing that would pop into anyone's mind when he passed away would be positive, something that his sister could be proud of, but at this point he doubted that would be the case.

In hindsight, he couldn't think of a single act he'd ever done that would be considered worthwhile to anyone other than himself. He had always felt invisible to those around him, blending into the woodwork when in a crowd, but now he realized it had been his own fault, not theirs. He'd never done anything of importance to warrant the recognition of others.

Dixie scratched at the door, so he stepped over to let her out. It seemed strange not opening up to Karen about something so important; she had always been the first person he confided in, but he'd never felt so empty and clueless before. Having been married to Sherry for over twenty-four years, he had a difficult time coping with the loneliness in her absence. Thank God for Dixie.

Derrick sat back on the sofa and picked up his iPad. There was no need to check emails since he didn't plan to respond anyway, but when he again saw the local news headlines on his Yahoo homepage, an updated one jumped out at him: *Accused Baxter Killer Pleads Not Guilty*. There was her photo again, captivating. This time he couldn't resist clicking on the link for the story:

> FLAGSTAFF, AZ—Larissa Baxter, accused murderer of her husband, Kenneth Baxter, pleaded not guilty today to all charges in a packed Flagstaff courtroom. Baxter has been free on bond since her arraignment September 23.
>
> The 36-year-old socialite claims to have been asleep in her bedroom when her husband was murdered outside her window.
>
> A spokesperson for the Baxter family states that they are actively assisting police in their investigation and vow that justice will be swiftly served at all costs. The Baxter family has been widely known throughout Coconino County over the past several decades for their numerous real estate development projects.
>
> Ms. Baxter was visibly shaken as she barely spoke above a whisper in response to Judge Clairmont's question, "How do you plead?"

A trial date has not yet been set.

Something clicked inside Derrick's head as he read the article. *Larissa Baxter? It can't be*, he thought. He massaged his forehead, straining to test his memory.

I've got to get in touch with George Garvin.

The contact info in his address book for George proved to be outdated. Both the telephone number and the email address were invalid. Yes, it had been several years since he'd been in touch with George, but people didn't just arbitrarily change their contact information these days.

Which precinct had George worked out of? He knew it was a Phoenix suburb—Tempe, Glendale, Scottsdale? They all ran together in his mind, but no one would likely remember George there anyway. He'd been retired from the force several years already when Derrick first met him years ago.

Finally, it dawned on Derrick to Google George's name. Following several clicks, the sad news struck him hard. An obituary stated that George had died a couple of years earlier.

Derrick hung his head. George had been a devoted pal while he struggled over health issues with Sherry, yet neither had made any effort to maintain the friendship after he'd moved back to Alabama. The loss now felt devastating. Derrick could clearly recall the conversation they'd had over beer and coffee in Williams near the Grand Canyon train depot. At the time Derrick thought George's comment was just the alcohol talking, but now it suddenly made sense.

The next day Derrick still agonized over George's concern for his daughter. This woman, Larissa Baxter, was likely innocent, yet the odds seemed heavily stacked against her.

He pulled up news clips from Flagstaff television stations and watched her being led away in shackles. He heard the tremor in her voice when a reporter asked if she had killed her husband and she denied it. She appeared emotionally and physically distressed, victimized by a system that was supposed to seek justice, yet in this instance the truth was unlikely to be served.

Another clip from the local news showed her defense attorney making a boilerplate comment about her innocence to a reporter. Larissa stood silently by his side, visibly shaking and tearful, she the Fay Wray to the justice system's King Kong. How could anyone think she was guilty?

Finally, he clicked on another link—a brief comment by the district attorney. "The State has decided not to pursue the death penalty," he stated. "However, life without the possibility of parole is entirely appropriate for this case."

Derrick couldn't imagine such a meek, petite woman behind bars with some of the state's most ruthless, drug-crazed felons. How could she possibly survive?

Deep in thought, he recalled one of his favorite Bible verses, Matthew 5:16: "Let your light shine before others, that they may see your good deeds and glorify your Father in heaven." Without question he knew why God had sent him back to Arizona: to save this woman from unjust prosecution and give her a second chance at life.

In that moment of awareness, Derrick felt an unusual warmth flow throughout his body. Despite his deteriorating health, he had a new purpose in life. He hadn't felt this good in years.

As Dixie barked at the sound of someone walking down the street past the house, Derrick decided that his stay in Arizona would be shorter than planned. He would find a way to save Larissa, even if it was the last thing he did; and it might very well be.

CHAPTER SIX

Flagstaff, Arizona

Larissa's address had been easy to find online, and Derrick drove past her house several times without seeing her. Positioned atop a wooded hill beyond a gated entrance, the almost palatial home was barely visible from the street. Google Maps clearly showed that her property bordered a nearby recreational area, so he decided that parking there and taking Dixie for a walk in the woods to the back of her house was a suitable plan.

That proved easier said than done. With no established trail leading toward her property, the vegetation was thick and difficult to traverse. Finally, he made his way to the rear of her property, only thirty or forty feet from her backyard swimming pool. He settled there with Dixie by his side, patiently watching and waiting for a glimpse of her to verify that he was indeed at the right place.

Derrick whispered a prayer that he was doing the right thing. Eventually it became evident that Larissa preferred to stay indoors by day, presumably to avoid news reporters and any public exposure. He returned to the same spot day after day, determined to see his mission through. Close surveillance helped him determine that she must be living alone, since he saw no evidence of other residents. While his daily backyard vigils dragged on, he wasn't discouraged like many people might be; the wait only fueled Derrick's desire to devote himself to doing something right with his life.

Larissa wasn't likely to do anything to help herself. She would simply be destroyed by the legal system. If there was a trial, she would lose; if she accepted any kind of plea bargain, she would still lose. The only way that she would get justice was through the intervention of a stranger.

Finally, on day four, Derrick watched Larissa drive away from her home, her face barely visible through the car's tinted windows only by virtue of an errant beam of sunlight through the sunroof. He now knew for certain that this was the right house and that she drove a dark gray Mercedes, so his surveillance would need to shift from the woods to nearby streets so he could follow her.

Driven by a deep compulsion, Derrick wasn't quite sure at this point how or when the execution of the plan first occurred to him. This woman needed him, and she didn't even know it. He was a complete stranger to her, yet her fate might very well rest in his hands. If he didn't act soon, it could be too late.

Derrick felt that he had experienced a catharsis of some kind. It would soon be time to leave Arizona and return to Alabama, cutting his trip much shorter than planned. Perhaps Larissa would accept his help; perhaps not. He would make every effort to give her the opportunity.

CHAPTER SEVEN

With each day of his vigil, Derrick grew more exhausted. His energy seemed to be slowly draining. After determining that Larissa had no regular daytime appointments, he decided to observe her at night. He followed her to a nearby health club and watched her go inside. Again, he was astounded by her beauty and peered from a safe distance through the front windows of the facility as the men in the gym gazed after her until she stepped out of view. Perhaps he'd been wrong in his assumption that she stayed behind closed doors by day to avoid public exposure. If she truly didn't want to attract attention, she wouldn't wear a tight-fitting sports bra and yoga shorts.

After all he'd been through with Sherry, he thought he'd never have such a reaction to a woman again, but with Larissa it was unavoidable, even though he didn't want to think of her in that way.

After observing her for several nights, he realized that Larissa followed a set routine, leaving for the gym at approximately the same time every other evening and returning home at around 9:00 p.m., except for an occasional stop at Starbucks. Now that her schedule was predictable, he knew when he could make his move.

Cottonwood, Arizona

As Derrick opened the front door of his rental cabin to finish loading the Tahoe for the trip home, he was struck by the bright, colorful Mexican designs painted directly onto the cabin's stucco walls in the living room. *You'd never see designs painted on walls back home,* he thought, and he would miss them. Glancing at a mirror mounted above the sofa, he stared blankly at his reflection. The man glaring back at him was almost unfamiliar, so much older than he felt inside, far more advanced than his actual age.

Taking a deep breath, then slowly releasing it, he was struck by his own mortality. Derrick was dying, yet no one knew, and it was time to give Karen the dreadful news upon his arrival back home. When he'd first received the confirming medical tests, he had been stunned. As it gradually sank in, he felt that he had little to live for anyway. The tragedy with Sherry had taken a lot from him, and he knew that no matter how intense his eventual physical pain might be, it couldn't match the emotional devastation he'd already experienced.

Strangely, however, as he became more accepting of his fate, Derrick almost seemed revitalized by the fact that he was now on a mission to save someone else who had a whole lifetime ahead of her. He would use his remaining time on earth to prolong hers—somewhat akin to an organ donor, at least in his mind. It didn't matter what eventually might happen to him if his rescue attempt failed or if Larissa refused him; there was that slightest connection with her father that inspired him. George was a good man, and Derrick regretted more than ever that he hadn't kept the friendship alive.

Perhaps Larissa would see him as some kook and turn a blind eye to the fact that he sincerely offered her a way out of her tragic predicament. If she refused and he ended up being arrested, so be it. He was dying anyway. What could they do to him? In his condition, the whole world was his prison anyway. In any event, at least now he could die in peace knowing that he had tried in his final days to do something right for a change. One good deed would make all the difference in the world to his dying state of mind.

He had estimated Larissa's height and weight and used an online chart to determine approximate clothing sizes for her, then he picked up a handful of plain print dresses and head scarves at a local thrift store. Tonight he would be on the road, with or without her.

With the cabin locked away and the key secured behind a coded lockbox, Derrick drove away from his Cottonwood respite for the last time, Dixie sitting up in the passenger seat beside him. He took a deep breath and wiped cold perspiration from his brow, then checked his watch. She would be returning home from the gym in a couple of hours, and he would be waiting for her.

Derrick held the crucifix suspended from his neck and said a silent prayer, then parked the Tahoe in the same spot as before in the recreational area, in close proximity to her house. He told Dixie to sit tight and left her in the car, grabbed a ski mask, revolver, and flashlight, then started the nighttime trek through the woods to the rear of the Baxter estate.

CHAPTER EIGHT

Crouched low to the ground behind some manzanita shrubs, Derrick took a deep breath beside the garage door to calm his nerves. It failed to help; his pulse quickened instead. A life-defining moment would soon occur when the headlight beams of Larissa's Mercedes bleached the darkness at the entrance of the long, winding driveway that led to her stately but isolated home.

Cicadas in nearby trees roared almost deafeningly; a quarter moon cast soft shadows across the adjacent driveway. Cold sweat broke out across his forehead and his heart pounded. In the eyes of the law he was about to attempt an unconscionable crime, but holding the crucifix dangling from a chain around his neck, he knew that God supported his actions. This plan was so out of character for him that it almost felt like a bad dream or an out-of-body experience. It wasn't too late to call it off. Could he really go through with such a bizarre scheme? Could his many days of preparation be only a pipe dream?

Clad in a navy sweatshirt, black sweatpants, and sneakers, Derrick had observed her leaving the health club only a short time earlier, and if she followed her usual routine, she'd drive straight home alone. He'd hurried away to get back to her house ahead of her and now waited behind chest-high vegetation at the farthest of three basement garage doors where he knew from previous surveillance she always entered. He was again surprised that no one, neither friend nor relative, seemed to be staying with her during her time of need.

A dog howled in the distance, or was it a coyote? A cool chill in the air brought shivers to his skin. Suddenly Derrick's hand started shaking. His back ached from stooping low to the ground, so he stood momentarily to stretch his legs. The wait seemed interminable; if she didn't arrive soon, he'd be forced to abandon the mission altogether. It was a crazy idea after all, he knew. Many might even consider him out of his mind. Perhaps he had become obsessed by her beauty. Maybe his attraction to her had tainted his original intent. There was something inexplicable that compelled him to take the most desperate action of his entire life.

The pleasant scent of pine carried by the slight breeze eased his nerves somewhat. Without a doubt he hadn't been himself lately. His whole world had recently been turned upside down with little to live for, so if he ended up in prison it would be no big deal. No one other than God could possibly understand what had driven him to this point, but he hoped she eventually would. He didn't want her to be an innocent victim of his madness, but—

Headlight beams suddenly bounced through the night from the gated entrance to her driveway, illuminating her majestic Tudor home. Motion-activated lights flashed on every twenty feet or so on both sides of the driveway as her car climbed the steep slope. *This is it*, Derrick thought. It was too late to back out now; she might see him running away and call the police. Besides, he had planned this carefully and couldn't imagine going back to the boring, mundane existence he'd been stuck in before the first time he saw her photo online.

Startled by a horned lizard skittering past his feet, he listened to the whishing rustle of pine needles in a nearby tree. The moon crept behind a cloud and left an even greater curtain of darkness. Perfect! He fumbled with the ski mask, sliding it over his face, exhaled deeply, and watched her car approach, closer . . . and closer.

The nearby garage door responded to the remote opener in her car and began to rattle upward. As the dim light of the ceiling-mounted unit inside the garage winked on, Derrick tried to recall what he'd intended to say to her when their eyes first locked, but in the stress of the moment his mind went blank.

Might she attempt to run? She looked so petite and diminutive on television, unlike anyone who could put up much opposition, but then again, he was quite a bit older than she, and he was weak. She was obviously in good physical shape, but hopefully she would still be exhausted from her workout, unable to physically avoid him until he stated his intentions. At this point, though, it didn't matter. The pistol in his pocket would be a much-needed equalizer and force her to listen. The operation had finally begun, and whatever happened would happen.

Derrick ducked closer against the brick wall behind the shrubbery to avoid being seen. It would take precise timing, but he'd practiced hiding and crawling several times while she was away. The moment was here. He was about to make the most bold move he could imagine—something he'd only seen in movies.

Her car made the final turn and slowly curved toward the garage door, the headlight beams sweeping across the shrubbery that concealed him. Momentary panic froze him in place, fearful that she might see his silhouette. Trying to slow his rapid heartbeat, Derrick took another deep breath and positioned himself for the critical move indoors when she punched the remote for the garage door to close.

Before he could even give it another thought, her car was parked inside and the door started to rattle down. He had to act quickly now; there was no turning back. Stooped low to the ground on his hands and knees, he crept from the shrubbery and crossed the threshold into the garage. Abruptly, the dropping door reversed itself and started to rise again. He'd forgotten about the safety sensor that prevented the door from striking anything when it came down. What else might he have miscalculated? His skin burned with nervous anticipation.

Squatting at the rear of her car, he sensed Larissa's hesitation inside. If she exited to investigate why the door re-opened, he would have to confront her while exposed to the outdoors, giving her the chance to run past him that he feared. He could never catch her. Her nearest neighbor was likely too far away through the woods to hear her scream, but perhaps he could corner her before that happened.

Derrick held his breath. A cold sweat rolled down his forehead. The agonizing moment seemed frozen in time, then finally the garage door began to rumble back down. He swallowed hard as the driver's door of her car swung open and her athletic shoes scratched against the floor's concrete surface. As he peeked around the rear of her car he saw a luxury SUV parked next to hers in the middle stall, and beyond that, to the left of the SUV, was a red sports car. He couldn't see enough of either to know for sure the make or model; he just knew that they were far out of his price range.

The time had come. He silently exhaled, stood, stepped around the rear of her car, and called out to her as she rose from the driver's seat, "Larissa!"

Her eyes bulged. She screamed and dropped her keys and purse to the floor.

"Larissa, I'm not here to hurt you."

She screamed again and backed away. "Stay away from me!" she shrieked.

Despite the intensity of the situation, Derrick couldn't help but marvel at her remarkable beauty. He'd seen her from afar at the gym, but up close she was stunning despite being terrified. Her dark brown hair tumbled lightly over her shoulders, her makeup flawless, not at all like someone returning from a vigorous workout. She was nothing short of spectacular. Her sparkling blue eyes were mesmerizing. She had to be wearing contact lenses; nobody's eyes could naturally be so blue. She wore the same tight, low-cut yoga shorts, purple in color, that hugged her curves and a matching low-cut sports bra. He couldn't remember having ever been in the presence of anyone even half as gorgeous as she .

He stepped toward her, his hands open wide, trying to appear nonthreatening. "This isn't what it seems. Please listen to me."

On an adjacent wall behind her hung a dart board, thankfully with no darts. By now she had backed against the rear of the garage where yard tools leaned against the wall. She grabbed a garden rake, swinging it wildly toward him. The rake slashed through the air, but missed, striking the driver's side window of her Mercedes with enough force to crack the glass.

"Please, Larissa, I'm only here to help you."

He removed the ski mask and tossed it to the floor.

She stared at him questioningly.

"I don't know you, and I don't need your help."

Derrick took another step toward her, and she swung harder, again missing and denting the hood of her car this time. The force of the impact jarred the rake from her grasp.

He stopped and slowly removed a snubnose .38 revolver from his pocket.

"No!" she screamed.

"Just listen, pl—"

"Please don't! Please don't!" she begged, tears streaming down her face. "I know who sent you, and I swear I didn't do it! I swear!"

Seeing her this way made him cringe with guilt. Larissa dropped to her knees, and he did as well. Derrick placed the revolver on the floor and slid it toward her. "I told you I'm not here to hurt you," he said. "Take this. You can hurt me if you want, but I would never harm you."

Suddenly the automatic light on the overhead garage door opener timed off, something else he hadn't planned for. As his eyes adjusted to the darkness, he heard her scrambling on the floor to retrieve the gun. Eerie rays of flickering blue from the dimly moonlit swimming pool outside reflected through a window and cast the garage in haunting waves of soft wavering light. Derrick reached into the other pocket and pulled out a small flashlight. When he flicked it on, she was on her knees aiming the weapon directly at him with a trembling, unsteady grip.

"Larissa, please listen to me."

"I told you, I didn't do it!" she screamed. Her breath grew more deep and rapid. The gun shook in her grasp.

"I know you didn't, Larissa, and no one sent me. I came here on my own."

He eased toward her, still on his knees, and watched her stabilize her grip on the revolver. Time stopped as if a pause button had been pushed; then, like slow motion, Derrick watched her finger tighten around the trigger and pull . . .

CHAPTER NINE

Larissa had a nagging headache as she drove home from the gym and felt dazed as she parked inside her basement garage, almost as if she were in a trance. Distracted by thoughts of what to wear at her next court appearance, the fact that the garage door had malfunctioned and started to rise after she closed it barely even registered in her mind. What had quickly jarred her back to harsh reality, however, was a masked man confronting her as she exited her car.

Her blood froze. Tears streamed down her cheeks; her heart pounded wildly. After all she'd been through, how could something like this be happening? She wondered why he had slid a gun toward her before the overhead light blinked out. He had to be deranged to give her such an easy way out. Regardless, she was determined to escape, so she fumbled in the dark to find the weapon on the floor. Fortunately, she was somewhat experienced with firearms, having gone to the firing range numerous times with her husband. This gun, however, was unlike any she had held. It was much heavier, so she grasped it awkwardly, her grip further complicated by the nervous shakiness generated by her fear. By the time her intruder aimed a flashlight toward her, she was ready and pulled the trigger.

Only a dull click sounded—no gunshot, no recoil, no acrid smell of gunpowder. The gun wasn't loaded; it had only been a cruel trick. She dropped it to the floor, it being useless anyway. Paralyzed with fear, she had to snap out of it and find another way to defend herself.

"Okay, Larissa, just hear me out," the man said. "Can we turn the lights on so I won't have to hold this flashlight?"

Nothing made sense. Was this a bad dream? What choice did she have but to listen to this raving maniac? Perhaps while he was talking she could figure a way out. If not, she could fake compliance, then find a way to escape when he eventually let his guard down. She remained silent as the stranger stepped to a nearby light switch and flipped it on. Four overhead fluorescent light strips buzzed to life down the entire length of the garage, bathing the space in starchy luminescence.

She backed against the wall behind her again and grasped a garden shovel this time.

"That's okay, Larissa, you can hold on to that if it makes you feel better. Just listen and I'll keep my distance."

She stepped toward him and swung, but missed again and retreated.

"It's okay," he said again. "You're in control here. I can't get near you without getting hit by your spade."

His voice didn't seem threatening, and neither did his manner. He was almost old enough to be her father, totally average and ordinary in looks, with a receding grayish hairline and a slight bulge around his middle. His physical condition appeared weak, and she could possibly best him if forced to. He didn't seem at all like a criminal; in fact, there was an element of kindness to his voice, something in his eyes, but how did that mesh with a revolver and a ski mask, not to mention the crucifix around his neck that her eyes kept returning to. He meant her no harm? *Yeah, right. Crazy guys like this are the most dangerous of all*, she thought. Her purse lay open on the floor. Could she keep him at bay long enough to get to it?

"Larissa, you don't stand a chance in court, and I'm offering your only way out."

Huh?

"If you don't get away from here, you'll spend years, if not the rest of your life, behind bars."

For some reason, despite the dire nature of her circumstances, the reality hadn't truly sunk in until now. He was right. All she'd been thinking about was a plea deal. Since she was innocent, it had never occurred to her what it would be like to actually live behind bars and that perhaps there might be another option.

"Look, I don't want anything from you, I promise," the man declared. "Maybe I have a knight-in-shining-armor complex, I don't know—I just want to save you from injustice. I can get you away from here to start a new life on your own, and you'll never see me again."

Larissa took a deep breath, shocked that she was seriously listening to him, but no; she couldn't allow him to talk her into something so farfetched. She glanced at the security alarm keypad mounted beside a mop and broom that hung from wall hooks above two wooden crates stuffed with paperbacks. Pressing the panic button on it would immediately call the police . . . if she could just get to it.

She slowly eased toward it, but the man glanced at the keypad and apparently figured out her plan. He stepped between her and the wall unit, then said, "Just listen to me, please. If you don't like what I say, you can push that button, I promise."

"But why are you doing this?" she asked.

"There'll be plenty of time to discuss that later," he said. "For this to work, we've got to get out of here fast. We need to get far away from Flagstaff where you won't be as easily recognized. You don't have a lot of time to decide."

He looked sad. Why did he seem so dejected and nervous? Was he actually giving her a choice?

"If you're under surveillance, we'll get caught. I don't think anyone has been watching you, though, or else I would have noticed. But even if you do get caught, you won't be any worse off than you are now."

She hesitated, and before she could say anything else, he continued nervously, "If you don't want to go, I'll leave and you can pretend this never happened. If you decide to go, though, I promise you this. If we get caught, you can claim that I kidnapped you, and I'll confess to it. It should give you more sympathy in the jury's eyes to have been taken against your will. Otherwise, you'll be seen as a fugitive. I really mean this, Larissa. I truly want to help you, but the decision is yours."

She rested the head of the shovel on the floor and held its handle to her side, then ran her fingers through her tussled hair. He seemed sincere. At the moment she felt both exhausted and dumbfounded. A trickle of perspiration rolled down her neck.

"I have a plan," he said. "If you'll just do as I say, I can get you hundreds of miles from here, and you can start your life all over without the threat of prison hanging over your head. You can leave this horrible mess behind you and reinvent yourself, find someone to love who'll treat you the way you should have been treated all along. You'll never hear from me again, I swear. This will be our form of justice, just between God and the two of us. It's only fair. I just want to help you."

He took a deep breath and pleaded with his eyes. "We can make this right, Larissa. It's the only way to make it right."

Now she started to weep; not the typical tears she had experienced since finding Ken dead in their pool, but loud, mournful sobs at the dawning realization of how bleak her situation truly was. She felt as if she was falling apart, more rattled than ever. Falling to her knees, she cried her eyes out. Was she having a nervous breakdown?

"Are you okay, Larissa?"

He stooped low and knelt beside her. She became unraveled and didn't even flinch or pull herself away. Perhaps it was the crucifix hanging from his neck that somewhat comforted her. Still, she felt helpless and alone, incapable of taking care of herself anymore. Here was the only person on the planet who believed in her, a complete stranger with a gun, and it felt good for a change not to be judged nor viewed as a criminal. In a moment of surrender she realized what she had to do. She would guard-edly put her fate in this man's hands. He was right; this was her only alternative. What did she have to lose? If he turned out to be a killer, well . . . she would rather die than go to prison anyway.

"What happens next?" she asked.

The semblance of a weak smile appeared across his face. "We set this up as a kidnapping," he said. "That's why I wore the ski mask. It has my DNA on it, but they don't have a sample to match it to. I've never been fingerprinted, so they can't match my prints either. They'll see the damage to your car when you swung the rake, so that's good. We'll need to knock some of these other garden tools around, too, as if there was a struggle, and I need to fire one shot to add to the realism. Then we need to drive your car to mine, switch to it, and get out of here."

It made sense, but she hesitated again. She was indeed put-ting her life in the hands of a complete stranger. He could be a smooth-talking sociopath with unspeakable motives for all she knew. While that was possible, one thing was certain; if she didn't take this chance, she would without question spend the rest of her life in prison, so she would undoubtably be rolling the dice between something bad or something worse. There was no good alternative here, only a risk.

Questions whirled inside her mind, but as he said, there was no time for those. She would watch his every move, and if she saw even a hint that he had ulterior motives, she would ditch him at the first opportunity. He didn't seem strong; in fact, he looked like he was falling apart. She was positive at this point that she could likely overpower him physically if she caught him by sur-prise without a weapon, should it come to that.

Larissa took a deep breath and exhaled. "Okay . . ." she re-lented. "Okay, but don't touch me."

She bent over and reached for her purse on the floor.

"No, Larissa, you can't take anything. You've got to leave it here. You've got to leave your whole life behind you."

"Even my makeup?"

"Yes! The cops will go through your purse item by item look-ing for anything that you might have taken with you. They'll try to determine if you ran on your own or if you had an accomplice or were actually kidnapped. We've got to make them think that you were—at least long enough to get you far enough from here so that no one will recognize you or suspect you."

She nodded. He was right. He was actually making sense; he had carefully thought this plan through.

Larissa picked up the gun from the floor and handed it to him. He quickly wiped away her fingerprints, loaded it, then stepped behind her and kicked several yard tools across the floor, firing a shot that hit the driver's side rear view mirror of her car. Could her nearest neighbor hear the shot through the heavily wooded estate-sized lots that separated them? she wondered. Probably not, but did it even matter? If this crazy plan were to work, she knew they had to leave undetected.

The man pocketed the gun and held out a hand for her. She refused to accept it, and he nodded. "Okay, sorry," he said.

He surveyed the room, apparently making sure that the scene reflected a kidnapping. "Oh, I almost forgot," he said. "Pick up the ski mask from the top and fling it backwards so it will look like you snatched it from my head. That'll put your DNA on it, too."

She complied. Finally he said, "Okay, get your keys and we'll drive to my car. We're wasting too much time."

Larissa obediently snatched her keys from the floor, sat in the driver's seat, and hit the remote door opener. As soon as the door was fully open, she started to back the car out of the ga-rage, hearing the crunch of her purse's contents as the front left tire ran over it. Once fully outside, she reflexively reached up to punch the remote for the door to close, but he stopped her. "No, don't," he said. "It'll look more like we left in a hurry if you leave it open."

Larissa felt a wave of nausea as she drove downhill past the motion lights along her winding driveway. It was too late to back out now. She was in it for the long haul.

When the Mercedes jerked to a stop behind the Tahoe, Dixie started to bark inside Derrick's SUV. Larissa reached for the keys but stopped after removing them.

"Throw them into the woods and leave your door open," Derrick said. "Hurry!"

As she started to exit the car, Derrick grabbed her right arm and said, "Wait. Before you get out, move your seat back as far as it will go so it will look like someone taller drove you here."

The whir of the power seat whined, then they rushed to the Tahoe, and Derrick opened the front passenger door for her. Dixie greeted her with a wagging tail and the canine version of a smiley face. "Larissa, meet Dixie," he said. Larissa, obviously still incredibly nervous, gave little response. "Dixie, back seat," he ordered the dog, motioning for her to move to the rear. Larissa climbed into the passenger seat and closed her door.

As Derrick started to drive away, Larissa said, "So I know your dog's name, but not yours."

Derrick gave a nervous laugh. The stress was getting to him, too. "I'm sorry," he said. I'm Derrick. Derrick Walton."

"And you're from Alabama?"

"Good guess. How did you know?"

"It wasn't much of a guess. Your accent gave you away when you first opened your mouth, and your car's license plate is from Alabama."

Derrick was taken aback by her blunt demeanor. "Of course," he responded, "you're right." He was accustomed to more genteel Southern women.

He noticed that she leaned as far away from him as possible, pressed against the passenger door. It was only natural, he thought. She still viewed him suspiciously, as she well should.

"I don't want to go to Alabama," she said.

Derrick shrugged. "I never intended for you to. We'll be traveling east on I-40. Amarillo and Oklahoma City are possibilities for you. I don't recommend Albuquerque, though. It's not far enough away from Flagstaff, and you could be recognized there."

He noticed her left hand shaking. She must still be in a state of shock.

"Larissa, I hope you'll—"

"Why are you doing this?" she interrupted him. "You said you would tell me."

Derrick cleared his throat. "Can't we wait for that explanation when we're both a bit more comfortable with this arrangement?"

"Don't expect me to get too comfortable," she snapped. "You're probably like all the others, only to a greater extreme."

"Others?"

Larissa sighed. "After my first appearance on the news, before I was a suspect, I started getting roses delivered to my door from strange men. Even after I was arrested and jailed, I got marriage proposals in my voicemail. Would you have done this for me if I looked more like a plain Jane?"

Derrick chuckled. "I can understand why you're so high on yourself. No one can deny how beautiful you are, but in truth your physical appearance worked against you in this case. I've put myself at risk in doing this, and one of my major strategies to avoid getting caught is to figure out how to disguise your good looks. If we don't do something to make you less noticeable, someone is going to spot you and call the cops."

She slightly shook her head at this comment. Derrick knew she wasn't convinced.

CHAPTER TEN

Eastern Arizona

Ahead, an eighteen wheeler's reflective emergency triangles glowed on the ground along the shoulder of the highway. Derrick shifted into the left lane and stretched as best be could behind the wheel. Having driven almost three hours already, he checked the dashboard clock. It was past midnight, and he was already more tired than expected, but he had no choice but to push himself to the limit.

"I've got to pee," Larissa broke the silence.

Derrick glanced in the rearview mirror at Dixie in the back seat. "Yeah, I need to walk Dixie, too," he answered.

Larissa shifted in her seat. "There's a gas station at the next exit."

Derrick took a deep breath and slowly exhaled. "We can't stop until we're ready."

"Ready for what?"

Derrick didn't answer. Instead, he motioned behind her seat. "There's a bag of clothes back there. Find a dress and slip it on over what you're wearing."

"What?"

"Just do it," he said, noting the confusion on her face.

She reluctantly reached back and brought the bag to her lap. The first item she removed was a denim shirtwaist dress, obviously secondhand, that would hang loosely around her body. "Do you really expect me to wear Amish clothes?"

"Larissa—"

"It probably hasn't even been washed!"

"There are scarves in there, too. Find one and wrap it around your head."

Larissa groaned and shook her head. "You're crazy if you think I'm—"

Derrick's temper flared. This situation was already far more stressful than he expected, and he couldn't help being irritable. He took a deep breath to calm his nerves, then softly said, "Larissa, I know all about you. I've read about you online. I know about your past."

She looked at him questioningly.

"I know that your entire life has been wrapped around your looks. Your physical beauty has gotten you into places that other women could only dream of. But your good looks are no longer an asset; they're a liability now."

Larissa appeared dumbfounded and shook her head. "I don't know what you're talking about, but—"

"Larissa, look at you. You're still wearing your workout clothes."

She scanned down the length of her body and shrugged.

"If any man sees you in that tight outfit, his eyes will bug out! If you want to stay free, you don't want to be noticed anymore. For the first time in your life you've got to play down your looks and pray that nobody gives you a second glance."

Larissa hung her head, then looked away.

"You're a fugitive, Larissa," he said. "Please get that through your head."

She blew out a pent-up breath, then pulled a scarf from the bag.

"But the colors don't even match!" she complained.

Derrick clutched the steering wheel tighter and gritted his teeth. "Okay, then why don't I just let you out at that gas station, and I'll go on my way. I want to be as far from here as possible when the cops arrive."

She lightly turned her head. "Would you really do that?"

He patted his right hand on the center console and glanced in the rearview mirror. Few cars were visible behind them on this isolated stretch of I-40. "I helped you get away, Larissa, but now you're endangering me."

"But would you really do that?"

"I told you, Larissa, that I don't want anything from you. There's no ulterior motive. I just wanted to give you a fair chance, and I've done that. But if you won't listen to me, this won't work. If you get caught, you've only dug yourself a deeper hole."

"But you said you would—"

"Yes, if I have to, I'll confess to kidnapping you, but that's the last thing I want to do. Right now I've got to drop you off safely somewhere, then I want to go home. It's that simple. But you're fighting me, and we'll get nowhere if we're not on the same page."

Dixie scratched at the back seat, obviously needing a break, and Derrick did, too.

After a moment of awkward silence, Larissa whispered an apology. "I'm sorry," she said. "You're right."

Without another word, she shrugged into the dress and wrapped the scarf around her head, then gazed at him with her dazzling blue eyes.

"Oh man," Derrick exclaimed, slowly shaking his head.

"What?"

He exhaled, shook his head, and mumbled, "You can't even ugly yourself up when you try to."

***

More comfortable after the restroom break, when they were back on the road, Larissa asked, "When will we stop and get some rest?"

"We need to get to the other side of New Mexico, as far as we can go before anyone discovers that you're missing."

She silently nodded.

"I have a room reserved at the La Quinta in Tucumcari. They accept pets there."

Larissa turned and stared out the passenger window into the night. The blinking red light atop a tall tower on a mountain seemed almost out of place in this stark rural wilderness.

"Larissa?"

"Yes?"

Derrick cleared his throat, then said, "This is only the beginning. There will be a lot about my plan that you won't like."

"So?"

"Just keep reminding yourself that no matter how bad you may think it is, it's a heck of a lot better than prison."

CHAPTER ELEVEN

Tucumcari, New Mexico

By the time Derrick and Larissa made it to their motel room at 5:00 a.m., they were too tired to do anything but sleep. It was a comfortable room with two queen beds and a flat-screen TV on the wall. Dixie slept on the floor between them. Derrick went for takeout food in the afternoon after they awoke. Larissa was in the bathroom when he returned.

"I hope you slept better than I did," he said to her through the closed door.

"I don't know what it's like to sleep well anymore," she answered.

Derrick paused for a moment, then said, "I'm sorry."

"For what?" she answered as she exited with a towel around her head and another plain dress on, this one falling well past her knees.

"For everything you've been through," he said.

Larissa sighed and sat on the edge of her bed. "I knew for a long time our marriage wouldn't end well. I just never would have expected it to be like this," she said.

Derrick handed her the diet drink she had requested and the bag of food he'd brought back. "Life happens," he said. "I guess we can all get hit with bad things that we never saw coming."

She unwrapped a grilled chicken sandwich and took a bite. Derrick pulled a burger from the bag and wolfed it down. He was starving. Dixie sniffed at the bag, and he removed a burger for her, too. It would be a couple of days at least before Dixie could get back to her regular diet.

Derrick paced around the room as Larissa combed through her wet hair with her fingertips. "I need to stop somewhere for some personal things," she said. "I don't even have a hair brush."

"Sure," Derrick said, "as soon as we're a safe enough distance away."

Suddenly a thought occurred to him. He took out his iPad and clicked on the bookmark for a Flagstaff TV station. On the news page there was no mention of Larissa's disappearance. If the police knew that she was gone, they hadn't released any information to the media. That was good. He and Larissa should be able to get even farther away before the story broke.

Derrick sat on the edge of his bed and watched Larissa try to push her hair into place. "Larissa, we need to have a serious talk before we leave here."

She looked up. "I'm listening," she said.

Derrick exhaled, trying to come up with the best way to explain the situation so she would accept what he had in mind. "When the cops find out that you're missing, they'll either label you as a fugitive or a kidnap victim," he said.

"Yes. We've discussed that already."

"Either way, it will be a national news story. It'll be sensationalized in all the newspapers, online, local TV, and radio reports everywhere. Photos of you will be all over the media."

"Why would you think that?"

Derrick rolled his eyes. At times she seemed rather dense, or at least not as sharp as he expected her to be. "Because you're a beautiful young woman and you're accused of murder. Are you a criminal or a victim or both? Your face will be recognizable everywhere. Your story will be so sensational that it will be almost impossible to keep your identity a secret."

"Hmm," she responded. "I thought you had a plan."

"I do, Larissa, and I think it's the only way we'll have a chance to get you through this, but you won't like it."

Derrick rummaged through his suitcase and brought out a pair of hair clippers. "We need to cut off your hair."

"WHAT?"

"All of it," he continued. "We need to make you look like a cancer survivor."

Larissa shook her head from side to side. "I can't believe this!" she said.

"But—"

"No! Absolutely not!" she said with an incredulous expression.

Derrick felt his anger rise again. It was unlike him to be so ill-tempered for the last day or so. "Are you so vain that you refuse to alter your appearance even at the threat of going to prison?"

"But there has to be another way."

"I'm listening," he said. "I'm open to any better idea that you can come up with."

A cool silence hung in the air until Derrick finally explained, "I tried hard to think of a better disguise, but I couldn't come up with one." He cleared his throat and looked her deep in the eyes. "Think about it." Derrick hesitated, choosing his next words carefully. "Everybody sympathizes with cancer victims, but they rarely make eye contact with them because it appears rude to do so. They generally look the other way when they suspect someone has been through chemo or radiation therapy."

Larissa slowly shook her head. "But that will destroy me. It's who I am."

"It's who you used to be," Derrick corrected her. "When I said that I wanted to give you a chance to start your life over, I meant just that, Larissa. You've got to kiss your old life goodbye. Instead of looking your best, you've got to try to look your worst."

"But that's crazy!"

"Is it?" He had to control himself to keep from speaking too harshly. "You can look pretty in prison or just average on the streets. Which do you prefer?"

It saddened him to see her so despondent. Was she truly capable of starting her life over from scratch? Perhaps he had overestimated her; at the moment he wasn't so sure that she could pull it off. "Which is it, Larissa?"

Tears streamed down her cheeks. "I wish I was dead," she said. "I can't do this. Maybe you could get me some pills or something, and I could just go to sleep and never wake up."

"I would never help you do that, Larissa," he said. "Life is precious. You have so much of it left, and you should appreciate that. You can still have a blessed life. I could never let you take the coward's way out."

She buried her face in her hands and quietly wept. Derrick wanted to hold her, to show her some compassion, but he was afraid it might be too much too soon and she might freak out. Instead, he tried to console her.

"It'll be okay," he said calmly, softly. "A year from now you'll be in a much better place. You've got some rough times ahead, sure, but nothing like life behind bars."

Dixie reacted to Larissa's tears by stepping up to her and laying her big head on the sobbing woman's lap. The sight of Larissa in such distress ripped Derrick's heart apart.

"I know you're having second thoughts," he said. "You're wondering if you did the right thing by running away." He paused and took a deep breath. "Believe me, I've had second thoughts myself. How in the world did I get involved in such a ridiculous plan? You don't know me, Larissa. You have no idea how out of character this is for me. Sometimes I feel like I don't even know myself anymore."

Larissa stroked her long shining hair.

"You're not guilty of anything, but I am," he continued. "I'm aiding and abetting a fugitive. People who know me would say that I would never do this in a million years. The only way this all makes sense to me is that it was meant to be."

She peered up at him. Her blue eyes had never looked less appealing as she obviously struggled with the whole concept. "Maybe I should just turn myself in," she said. "I could say that I was kidnapped, but that I was blindfolded and tied up the whole time. I wouldn't say anything about you, I promise."

Derrick sat beside her on the bed, the closest he'd been to her yet, feeling a mysterious connection between himself and her. "We're in this together, Larissa," he said. "If you go to the police, I go with you."

Dixie whined, apparently uncomfortable with the drama unfolding before her. Larissa glanced around the room in unmistakable deep thought. "You're really not one of those kooks who sent me flowers," she said. "You're a real man. I've never known many of those."

With a deep sigh she pointed to the clippers and said, "Let's get this over with."

CHAPTER TWELVE

The Texas Panhandle

It was just after dark when the Chevy Tahoe crossed the state line into Texas. Derrick felt it would be far safer to drive at night when fewer travelers mingled at rest areas and stopovers to refuel.

He glanced at Larissa, saddened by her new appearance. Cutting her hair had been like trimming the petals from a beautiful flower, but she would be much less recognizable now in her faded dress, closely-cropped hair, and scarf. Without makeup she looked frail and vulnerable, as if she were indeed a cancer survivor. Her demeanor reflected a change as well. While she seemed more comfortable with him, she also appeared insecure as she no longer hid behind stylish clothes and mascara.

"Are you okay?" he asked as she stared blankly out the passenger window into the dark of night.

She didn't respond immediately but finally admitted, "Yes, I guess. About as well as anyone could be under these circumstances."

Derrick nodded, noting how fidgety she had become. "We'll be passing through Amarillo soon. Have you thought about where you'd like to be dropped off?"

Larissa exhaled deeply. "Actually, I haven't. Everyone I know lives in the opposite direction."

Derrick felt a growing frustration. How could he get her to understand what lay ahead for her? "Larissa," he said, "you can't get in touch with anyone you know anyway. The FBI will monitor every friend and relative you have, thinking that if you're a fugitive rather than a kidnap victim, you'll contact someone close to you for help. Like I told you, you've got to start all over. A totally clean slate."

"I know what you said," she snapped, "but don't you see that that's a whole lot easier said than done? How does anyone with absolutely nothing to her name establish herself in a new place and start all over? You're expecting me to think like a criminal on the run, and that's not what I am. I'm honestly not sure that I can do it. I didn't think this through enough. I've probably made a huge mistake."

Derrick understood. He wasn't even sure that he could pull it off himself if the roles were reversed, but what did she have to lose? "You know, it really wasn't such a big decision for you. What was your alternative? If you decide to give yourself up, you won't be any worse off than before."

She didn't comment. For a moment Derrick regretted putting her in this predicament.

"Look, you don't have to choose a place along I-40. I'll take you anywhere you want to go. Dallas could be nice; we could make a detour there. Is there any other place that's ever appealed to you more than others?"

"STOP IT!" she said in a raised voice between gritted teeth. "Can't you see that the place doesn't matter? It'll be just as difficult in Dallas as it would be in Oklahoma City! I don't care! I can't even think straight anymore; how can I just show up somewhere and be automatically accepted?"

Derrick knew it was time to drop it. What could he do now? This obviously wasn't going to work. He wanted to tell her that, with her good looks, it wouldn't be difficult to attract a man who would support her, but her appearance was still a sore issue so soon after she'd chopped off her hair.

"What will I do to survive?" she continued. "I don't have much education. Will I work in a diner somewhere? Where will I live? I just don't care anymore. Prison doesn't sound as bad as it did before."

For a moment it dawned on Derrick how far-fetched this plan had been to begin with. He also wondered, now that he was in the thick of it, how Larissa's actions could impact him personally. He could end up being a major embarrassment back home. How might Karen feel? First he'd withheld the news from her that he was dying, then his face could be plastered all over the news for helping a fugitive escape justice. Karen would have to watch him die behind bars. She would feel so ashamed and disappointed. He had had good intentions for Larissa, and it had seemed plausible at the time. Larissa said that she hadn't thought things through enough. He obviously hadn't either. Still, he had done his best. No matter what, though, he wouldn't give up on her.

"Derrick . . ." she said. "I'm scared. I'm really scared."

"Anyone would be," he responded with a nod.

"This is crazy," she said. "You were crazy for coming up with this idea, and I was crazy for going along with it."

Derrick nodded again. "You're right. I can't argue with you there." He paused briefly, noticing the flashing red lights of an approaching police car in the rearview mirror. He tensed and held his breath, then finally felt an enormous sense of relief when the emergency vehicle sped past them. He swallowed hard, then said, "But what's done is done. We can't change anything now, so I guess we'll just have to be crazy together."

She sniffled and appeared nervous once again. This whole rescue was supposed to have made him feel better about his own life by focusing on someone else's. Instead, he felt like he very well could have screwed up an innocent person's life as well as his own.

"I don't want you to do anything that you're uncomfortable with," he said. "It's your life, Larissa, and you need to cherish it. No one knows that better than I do. I hope you won't waste yours, but whatever you decide, I'll be beside you. Don't let yourself feel alone anymore. We'll figure something out, and I'll be with you until you're ready to tell me goodbye."

Having located the closest police station with his cell phone while waiting for Larissa at the last rest stop, Derrick left the interstate at Exit 141, drove into McLean, Texas, and pulled into an old historic Phillips 66 service station to park. A state police office was only a few blocks away.

The small town seemed deserted at this hour. A blinking yellow caution light swung above a nearby intersection in the stiff wind. Larissa trembled, feeling vulnerable and insecure. She watched him sheepishly and said, "I'm sorry, but, honestly, there's no need for you to go with me. Just drop me off."

Derrick cleared his throat. The mood was ominous. Dixie stuck her head between the two front seats as if she wanted to listen in on the conversation. Massaging his forehead with his fingertips, Derrick said yet again, "I don't feel good about this, but, like I told you, if you go, I go."

Larissa twisted in her seat to face him and admonished him, "Don't be so stubborn. You shouldn't put yourself through this." A squad car passed, traveling in the direction of the police station. Larissa cringed as she ducked down in her seat, second-guessing herself about giving up so easily.

"If a cop sees you obviously hiding from him, he'll investigate; then voluntarily giving yourself up won't be an option," Derrick warned. "It'll play out better for you if you turn yourself in rather than get caught."

Larissa stared at Derrick sympathetically and realized in that moment that she couldn't do this to him now. There would be plenty of other opportunities to surrender along the road ahead; perhaps it had been a rash decision for only her second day on the run. She should first give it more thought.

Derrick hung his head, sadness written all over his face. For some inexplicable reason, her freedom meant a lot to him. He had put himself at risk for her, had been the only person to believe in her. Now she suddenly had a complete change of heart. Larissa leaned back in her seat, exhaled, then said, "Let's get back to the freeway. The timing doesn't feel right for this."

Before Derrick could respond, the flashing blue lights of a police cruiser pulled up beside them. Larissa froze as Derrick put the driver's side window down. The police officer lowered his passenger side window and shined a flashlight at them, first at Derrick's face, then Larissa's, and finally at the loaded cargo space.

"You folks can't park here, sir," the officer said.

Larissa's left hand squeezed Derrick's right knee. She felt his tension.

"Yes, Officer," Derrick responded. "I was . . . looking for a gas station that's open."

The light moved back into Larissa's face and almost blinded her. "Who's this?" the officer inquired.

"Uh . . . my daughter. I . . . uh . . . picked her up in Amarillo to take her back home to Alabama for more chemo."

Dixie surged forward from the back and stuck her head out of the driver's window next to Derrick, who pushed her back to the rear seat.

The officer's hesitation was maddening. Thoughts swirled through Larissa's head. What was he thinking? Had he recognized her? She felt Derrick's right leg shaking, from nervous tension, no doubt.

"Go east on First Street, then take a left onto Rowe," the officer suggested. "If the Food Mart isn't open, there's a Shell station on Exit 142."

"Yes, thank you, Officer," Derrick said as he put the Tahoe into reverse. When he backed out to go around the police car and return to the street, Larissa noticed that the cop still stared at them. Would he follow them and pull them over again?

With a sigh of relief, Derrick followed the main street through the center of town, watching for a sign directing them back to I-40 and Exit 142. Fortunately, the squad car remained parked. Larissa looked at Derrick incredulously. "What?" she said. "You're not even going to try to talk me out of changing my mind?"

She had yet to see such a broad grin on his face. "Nope!" he said. "Not on your life!"

CHAPTER THIRTEEN

Western Oklahoma

The rest of the night seemed endless ahead of them.

Putting the aborted surrender behind her, Larissa still felt restless. She'd never been on an extended road trip, and this one came under the worst conditions imaginable. She took a deep breath to relieve her nerves, then decided to start up a conversation. "You're not wearing a ring, so I assume you're not married?" She noticed an immediate change in his expression, a face of sheer sadness.

"No, not anymore," Derrick answered, swallowing hard and shifting in his seat.

Recognizing that he obviously didn't want to talk about it, she promptly changed the subject. "Why did you scare me to death instead of just introducing yourself and explaining your plan?"

With a nod Derrick glanced at her. "I considered that," he said, "but I decided that I needed to get your attention quickly and get you out of there fast. If we had had a more social conversation, it would have taken a lot more convincing, and we didn't have time for that."

"Okay, I'll buy that, but I don't understand the gun thing. What was that all about?" she asked.

"Huh? What?"

"Why did you give me an unloaded gun? What was the purpose of that?" Larissa asked.

Derrick raised his brows. There was that smile again. He almost seemed embarrassed. "It was supposed to have been a test," he explained.

"How's that?"

Derrick laughed softly. "I thought I had all the answers," he said. "I figured that if you just held the gun on me and let me explain, I had a pretty decent chance of talking you into leaving with me. But if you pulled the trigger, it would mean that you would need a whole lot more convincing and that maybe I should just make a run for it."

"But you didn't."

"No, I didn't."

"Why not?"

Derrick ran nervous fingers across his thinning scalp. To the right side of the highway shoulder a bent-over mile marker sign had apparently been struck by a vehicle at some point. "It's hard to explain," he finally answered, "but I've been consumed with planning your rescue for a while now. I wanted to do something good with my life, to help someone in need. It was important to me personally and spiritually. So even though you pulled the trigger, at that moment I just couldn't give up on you. Not without trying one more time to help you see that it was your only chance."

Silence filled the night. A coyote trotted across the highway in front of them, and Derrick tapped the brakes.

"There's something you should know," Larissa said.

"What's that?"

"You startled me when I got out of the car, and I dropped my purse," she said.

"So?"

"There was a gun in it. If I hadn't dropped it, I would have shot you."

Derrick looked stunned. "Really?"

"Of course I would have. You were a masked intruder. What would any armed woman have done?"

Derrick shook his head. "Wow!" He exhaled deeply. "Guess I wasn't as smart as I thought I was."

Silence consumed them until Derrick asked, "What did you mean when you said 'I know who sent you'? Who did you think sent me?"

Larissa shook her head. "Isn't it obvious? The Baxters, Ken's mom in particular. She hated me from the beginning. Convicting me and sending me to prison wouldn't have been enough for her. She would have loved to have seen me dead."

"Do you think she's really that convinced of your guilt?"

Larissa gave a sarcastic laugh. "Guilt or innocence probably doesn't even matter to her. With her son in the grave, she'd like to see me there, too, whether I killed him or not."

She closed her eyes for a moment and tried to get a grasp again for the thousandth time on why this all happened and how she ended up in a car with a stranger speeding away cross-country. "Why were you so convinced that I was innocent when everyone else was ready to put me away? I still don't understand. That's why I felt that you were just obsessed with me physically and wanted me for . . . *that*. I figured it didn't really matter to you if I was guilty or not."

Derrick looked at her through the dim glow of the dashboard lights, a certain kindness visible in his expression. "It wasn't that at all," he said. There was an awkward pause, then he added, "Oh, I was attracted to you, all right. Any man would be. But that had nothing to do with wanting to help you."

"But that doesn't answer my question. Why did you think I was innocent?"

"Fair enough. Let me tell you a story."

"I'm listening."

"Well, several years ago my wife's allergies got worse. My web development business was doing well, and I could work from anywhere, so we decided to move to Arizona temporarily to see if the dry climate helped. We found a nice rental place in Sedona. We loved the area, but it was a bit pretentious for us. Plus, after several weeks Sherry felt a little better, but not enough to stay. She got homesick and we missed Alabama."

Larissa's attention began to wander. *Where was he going with this?* she thought. Derrick seemed to have a problem getting to the heart of any story.

"One day there a knock on the door. It was a retired police officer helping a friend on a cold case. He needed to interview Derrick Walton. He had found the right name but quickly realized that I was the wrong man. Anyway, there was an instant chemistry between us, and we became fast friends. His name was George Garvin."

"Daddy?" she said. "I had a feeling that's where this might be leading. He had an over-the-top personality." Tears welled in her eyes.

"Yes, he did," Derrick agreed. "After that, we met occasionally for lunch here and there. I loved hearing his stories. I drove down to the Phoenix area a couple of times or met him when he was in my area. He had a long list of people to question about his investigation, and they were scattered all over the state.

"When I first saw the headlines and your photo on my iPad, something in the back of my mind clicked, but I dismissed it pretty quickly. When I read a news piece later and saw your name and the family you were married into, I immediately remembered a particular conversation with George."

Larissa sniffled and wiped her eyes. "I miss him so. He would be my number one supporter if he was still here."

"There's no doubt about that. He was seriously concerned about you when I knew him."

Derrick became distracted momentarily as an oncoming vehicle failed to dim its headlights. He squinted until his eyes readjusted to darkness.

"We met for coffee in Williams near the depot. He needed to question someone who worked on the Grand Canyon train, and it was about an hour before it returned. That day all he talked about was you. He said he knew that you weren't nearly as happy as you pretended to be and was upset that you seemed to be keeping things from him."

Larissa hung her head. He had been right.

"George had done some snooping around about your husband—what was his name again?"

"Ken."

"Yeah, Ken. George was convinced that you were only a trophy wife to Ken and that he would give you up in a heartbeat if it served him better. He also said that Ken's family never accepted you, that they looked down on you behind your back."

"And not always just behind my back," she interrupted.

"Anyway, what had him particularly upset that day was that he had talked to a former friend of Ken's. I forget his name. This guy told George that he had been set up by Ken's family. They had thrown him under the bus to protect Ken. It might have been drug-related, I can't remember. He more or less said that the Baxter family would stop at nothing to protect their image. George was more angry than I'd ever seen him, and he said something to the effect that if you didn't get out of that marriage, someday you'd be their scapegoat, too, and now here you are."

Between sobs, Larissa managed, "He said something similar to me once. It must have been after your conversation with him. I was so caught up in my life of luxury that I refused to listen. I denied everything and told my dad to mind his own business. I've always regretted those words. It wasn't long after that that his health started to fail."

"Well, that's what brought me here."

Larissa stared blankly ahead into the night. "But that's not much to go on, Derrick, to put yourself at such risk. You still can't know for sure that I'm innocent."

Derrick swallowed hard, then asked, "Well then, did you?"

"What?"

"Kill your husband."

Larissa laughed, then sighed. "Of course I didn't, but not because I didn't want to. I just didn't have the guts."

"Where will we stop to sleep?" Larissa asked. "I'm exhausted." In addition to being mentally stressed, she felt physically fatigued as well. She'd never been so sleep deprived.

"We'll get some rest at a La Quinta in Arkansas; Russellville, I think it is."

"What time do you think we'll get there?"

Derrick looked at the time display on the dashboard. "Probably four or five in the morning, depending on how long we stop for food and restroom breaks," he answered.

"Would you like for me to drive a while? I know I should have offered sooner, but—"

"I'd love for you to drive, but there's no way. You don't have a driver's license, and if we were stopped for even a minor violation, we'd be sunk."

"Oh . . . right."

Larissa shifted in her seat. She'd been silently considering possibilities and might have come up with a short-term solution, depending upon Derrick's approval.

"Derrick . . ." she began.

"Yes?"

She felt nervous revealing what she was thinking, not wanting him to get the wrong impression. Despite the fact that he seemed safe and true to his word, she didn't want to play into his hands in case he did have a dark side. After all, he was still a complete stranger, and a man. She had been accustomed throughout her life to men targeting her for their own selfish needs. For now, though, she saw no other way out.

"Would you . . . would you mind if I went with you to Alabama . . . just for a short while?"

Derrick shrugged, his surprise evident. "Changed your mind, huh?" He was obviously taken aback. "Are you sure?"

Relieved that he hadn't immediately rejected the idea, she explained, "I feel like I'm in such a rush making decisions that will affect the rest of my life. I'd just like to have more time to think."

She watched his facial expression brighten and wished she could read his mind. "I totally understand," he finally said. "We'll just have to think of an excuse to explain who you are and why you're there. Contrary to what people in other parts of the country may think, we do have running water and electricity in Alabama. Your story will be just as visible there as anywhere else." Derrick scratched his head in apparent thought. "But it's a smart idea. You can take as long as you want. I like your plan. It takes the pressure off both of us, for now at least."

Her face beamed with instant relief. "I've never been to Alabama," she said, "but I have ancestors from there."

"Really?"

"Yes, they came to Tombstone during the silver rush. I have roots in the Wild West."

"That's fascinating," Derrick responded, but his attention was diverted when he had to swerve to dodge a crossing armadillo.

Larissa didn't know what to say next. She was tired of talking. Road signs indicated the distance ahead to Oklahoma City, and she felt a minor sense of relief. Hopefully with this temporary decision out of the way, she'd finally be able to get some rest when they stopped in Arkansas.

Dixie began to whimper. She needed a break, and Larissa did, too.

"I know, I know," Derrick said. "We all need to stop. I think there's a rest area not too far ahead."

Relaxing behind the steering wheel as they entered Arkansas, Derrick yawned, then said, "Tell me something good."

Larissa glared at him in the dim light and answered incredulously, "Are you kidding me?"

Derrick smiled at her, feeling more at ease now that their destination was clear. "No, I'm not. There's always something good."

Shaking her head, Larissa snapped, "I'm running for my life. Nothing's good."

"You're not in jail, right? That's good."

Larissa sat silently, apparently distancing herself from the conversation.

"You're beautiful, you're healthy, and you have a long life ahead of you. That's good, isn't it?"

Larissa sat silently. "Humph," she finally responded, flipping down the sun visor to stare at her reflection in the mirror behind it, her image barely visible in the low light. "Just look at me. You can't possibly call this beautiful."

With a laugh Derrick shot back, "I told you before that you can't hide your looks. Besides, your hair will grow back and you'll laugh at this conversation."

Larissa groaned and snapped, "So what's good for you, Mr. Glass Half Full?"

Another big grin spread across Derrick's face. "That's easy," he said. "I'm going home!"

CHAPTER FOURTEEN

Russellville, Arkansas

The two travelers quickly grew tired of fast food, but Derrick thought their safest option to maintain Larissa's low profile was to make best use of drive-throughs.

Before they checked in at the motel, Derrick decided to refuel so they could get a quicker start that night on the final leg of their journey. To save time, Larissa offered to go to the restroom, then walk Dixie while Derrick pumped gas. Since they were now far from Flagstaff and she was heavily disguised, he decided it should be safe. His energy zapped from another long day of driving, he wanted to get to the motel as quickly as possible.

Watching Larissa lead Dixie through a grassy area as he stood at the gas pump, Derrick again noted that she couldn't just blend in to her surroundings, no matter how hard she tried. Perhaps she still looked striking to him because he knew what lay beneath her baggy clothes, but in a few moments he noticed another man pumping gas glaring at her.

Derrick grew more and more uncomfortable and decided to forego cleaning the windshield to immediately get her back into the car. He stopped the pump short of a fill-up, then quickly stepped to her side and whispered, "Somebody's staring at you too long. You need to get back into the car so we can get out of here." She nodded her consent, and within minutes they were back on the road in search of the La Quinta, only a couple of blocks away.

Before settling in for the night Derrick brought out his cell phone and glanced at the adjacent bed where Larissa had collapsed moments earlier. "Hey!" he said. "I'd like to take a picture of you."

Larissa sprang to a seated position on the mattress and in obvious shock answered, "ABSOLUTELY NOT! Are you kidding? I would never want anyone to see me like this!"

Exhausted also, Derrick realized this was a battle not worth fighting, but he would truly like to have photos to document this important mission.

"Why didn't you take my picture before I looked like . . . *this*?" she continued. "I look like a pioneer woman out on the prairie! You don't know me well at all if you think I'd let anyone take a picture of me like this! It was bad enough getting my mug shot taken."

Following a brief pause, Derrick put his cell phone away and collapsed onto his own bed. "You look beautiful either way," he said softly.

Dixie barked twice at the sound of other travelers talking outside, and moments later Larissa was sound asleep. Although he was exhausted from a second long night of driving, there was no way that Derrick could get any sleep without first checking on the latest developments back in Flagstaff. Larissa awoke briefly and pulled a pillow over her head, while Dixie had taken her position on the floor between the two queens. Derrick logged onto his iPad and found the web page of the Flagstaff TV station he had frequented before. There it was, the lead story. He clicked on the link and watched.

An attractive blonde reporter stood holding a microphone at the bottom of Larissa's driveway with yellow crime scene tape strung across the gate visible in the background. A lone police officer stood guard, and farther off, flashing red and blue squad car lights were visible up the hill.

"Flagstaff police report that Larissa Baxter, charged with murdering her husband, Kenneth Baxter, is missing," the reporter announced. "Baxter's defense attorney, Harvey Bateman, discovered an open garage door and disarray inside when he called on his client for a consultation this afternoon. Flagstaff police confirm evidence of a possible struggle; however, they haven't ruled out the possibility of a staged crime scene. Baxter was last seen two nights ago when leaving Flagstaff Athletic Club's east location on North Country Club Road.

"Ms. Baxter had been released on bail and was awaiting trial. At this point in the investigation, authorities refuse to speculate if Baxter is an actual kidnap victim or a fugitive.

"The FBI has been called in to assist and have set up surveillance at the Nogales border crossing."

A full image of Larissa's mug shot filled the screen.

"If you see this woman, please notify your local authorities immediately."

Derrick powered the iPad down and fell back onto the bed. His skin tingled from nerves. It was official and would be a different game now. He glanced at Larissa in the dim glow of the bedside lamp. How could anyone believe she was guilty of such a horrible crime? Admittedly, he didn't know her well, but she had a terrific father. It was hard to imagine George raising anyone who wasn't a law-abiding citizen.

Switching off the lamp, Derrick tried to relax and hoped he would get more sleep than the past couple of nights. Exhaustion had completely worn him down.

CHAPTER FIFTEEN

Eastern Arkansas

A driving rain pounded the windshield as the Tahoe headed east once again a couple of hours past sunset. Larissa, dressed in her typical garb, hadn't complained about her appearance since he'd explained the dire need to disguise herself.

She gave him a curious look and asked, "Are you okay?"

He didn't answer right away, reluctant to give her the news. Finally, he told her, "It's all over the news. We're officially fugitives."

She rolled her eyes. "And that surprises you?" she asked.

"Of course not. It's just . . ." He took a deep breath, then wiped fog from the windshield. The defroster wasn't as effective as it should be. "I've never been in trouble my whole life. I've only had one speeding ticket, and that was decades ago." His skin tingled and burned, as if it were on fire. He hadn't expected to have such a nervous reaction.

Several moments of silence passed before Larissa finally responded, "I can believe that. I don't know you all that well, but you seem like a straight shooter to me." She twisted in her seat to look through the back window, then said, "Any friend of my dad's would have to be okay."

He felt himself growing even more edgy as the realization struck home that he truly was on the run from the FBI even though the feds didn't yet know it. He actually could go to prison for the rest of his life, how little of it might be left anyway. To calm himself, he thought about home and knew he would feel safer and more at peace there, then he changed the subject.

"I read about you online," he said. "You don't seem the type to have been a stripper."

"Showgirl," she corrected him.

"Showgirl?" he said. "What's the difference?"

"I was never completely nude," she answered in a sarcastic tone.

"So, were you in one of those Vegas floor shows or in a club of some kind?"

Larissa sighed. "Do we have to talk about this?"

"I'm just curious about how you ended up where you are now. George never told me much about his own personal life, much less yours. He was mainly upset about your in-laws."

Larissa sighed and stared blankly ahead. "When I was nineteen, my mom left my dad. Being the wife of a cop had taken its toll on her."

"I've always heard that being the wife of a cop can be difficult."

"I loved my dad, but he was married more to his work than to my mom. She sort of flipped out and moved to LA. We were never close after that."

"So you stayed behind with your dad?"

The brake lights of stopping cars ahead glowed brighter as he brought the Tahoe to a halt. A driving rain pounded the hood of the SUV, a perfect storm for automobile accidents. The roar of the rain made it difficult to hear.

"No, I didn't stay with Dad," she answered. "Our family split up in different directions. That's when I left for Vegas with stars in my eyes. I was going to become a sensation there, then move on to Hollywood."

Derrick nodded, keeping his eyes focused on the road. "It apparently didn't work out that way."

With a soft moan and a shake of her head Larissa explained, "Vegas was full of beautiful girls. I didn't stand out any more than any of the others."

A flash of lightning and subsequent rumble of thunder rattled the car. "Hmm. George didn't know that you were a . . . showgirl, did he?"

"As far as I know he didn't. I told him I managed a restaurant. He was so involved with his work that he never once came to see me, so it was an easy cover-up."

"So, I assume Ken was a customer at your club?"

Larissa slowly nodded. "He was there constantly and became infatuated with me, even a pest at times. He was an okay looking guy and was obviously well-off. We hadn't been seeing each other long before he proposed to me. It was a no-brainer to accept."

"But it didn't go well with his family?"

"Are you kidding? A Baxter marrying a Vegas showgirl? They tried everything possible to stop the marriage. With no support from his family, we eventually gave up on big wedding plans and got married in a Vegas chapel."

"I'm sure that must have been difficult knowing that his family was against you from the start."

Larissa removed the scarf from around her head, revealing the short stubble of her scalp. "I don't need to wear this now. We're obviously not stopping anytime soon." Traffic slowly inched forward at less than ten miles per hour. "Anyway, it's night, and even the car next to us can't see clearly through all of this rain."

Derrick nodded his approval. He checked Google Maps on his cell phone and noted with relief that the heavy traffic should be clearing soon.

"Ken's parents even called me a gold digger to my face," she continued, "and the truth is, I guess I was. I was seduced by his lifestyle, not by him."

"So did you have regrets?"

"Of course I did! I was miserable from the start! As the old saying goes, money can't buy happiness, and I would testify to that any day."

"But you must have said something about it to George for him to know as much about your situation as he did."

"Don't kid yourself. Yes, I talked about it some, but it was his snooping around that brought the truth of the matter to light. He was determined to protect me whether I wanted him to or not."

"Why didn't you leave Ken and go back to Phoenix?"

"His family may not have approved of our marriage, but they were even more opposed to divorce. They wanted the Baxters to be viewed by the world as perfect, at any cost. Baxters don't make mistakes. I was stuck. They would have destroyed me."

Larissa looked incredibly sad, but she had every right to be having been falsely accused of a felony, a situation that few women ever faced. She had had a miserable life, and even the promise of a new existence failed to excite her. Overall, Derrick felt that she was holding up rather well. Hers was a world of darkness, where by comparison his life had been full of love regardless of his own hardships.

Larissa changed the subject. "Where will we stop for rest this time?" she asked.

Derrick accelerated gradually as the car ahead moved faster. "Well, tonight, my dear, we'll be in sweet home Alabama at my place on the lake. No more motels."

Larissa gave a half-hearted laugh. "It'll be nice to get out of this car, but then I guess the next challenge will be explaining who I am to everyone you know."

Derrick swallowed hard and felt a sense of sadness about his own life as reality set in. "That may not be too difficult," he said. "I don't have any close friends. I'm basically a loner. It'll just be my sister who we'll need to convince. That won't be easy, though. She's pretty sharp."

Larissa stared out the passenger window at distant flashes of lightning. "Are you close to your sister?" she asked.

"Very much so."

With a sigh she answered, "I've always wondered what it would have been like to have a sibling. Guess that's something else I missed out on."

A putrid odor suddenly overwhelmed their senses.

"Eww, what in the world is that awful smell?" Larissa asked with a wrinkled nose.

Derrick laughed. "It's a skunk," he answered. "Some old-timers in the South call them polecats."

Bringing both feet up to the front edge of her seat and wrapping both arms around her knees, Larissa smirked and commented, "Well, if you've got polecats in Alabama, you can take me back to Arizona."

"Well, I'll have you know," Derrick responded with a grin, "you've got 'em there, too."

The traffic in Memphis was light as they passed through in the early hours of morning before rush hour. When they entered Mississippi, Derrick felt like he was almost home. There was something about the South that was almost indescribable.

Daylight approached, and he was determined to drive the rest of the way home regardless. He would take extra precautions in the light of day, but they were so far from Flagstaff now that the chances of anyone recognizing Larissa were minimal, especially under her masquerade.

CHAPTER SIXTEEN

Talladega County, Alabama

At almost 10:30 a.m. the Tahoe rolled across Stemley Bridge, the Coosa River below a much-welcomed sight to Derrick. Only a few more miles and he would be home again, where he would be relieved of the jitters and live his final days in peace.

Taking a deep breath, Derrick wanted to absorb the entire environment—except for the accumulated candy wrappers and crumpled fast-food bags on the floorboard. Larissa was slumped in the passenger seat, asleep. Dixie perked up, and he could almost get a sense that she knew exactly where she was, excited also to be at home.

Within minutes Derrick brought the car to a stop in his driveway. With so few houses occupied year-round along the shoreline, the area was eerily quiet. With summer now almost a distant memory, the sky was cloudy, and a late morning fog still hung over the Logan Martin waters.

Derrick yawned, then exhaled as he sat behind the steering wheel listening to the cooling tick of the engine. The journey might be over, but what remained ahead was perhaps an even greater challenge. It all seemed like a dream except for the fact that Larissa was still with him. The more demanding task of maintaining her anonymity would now begin, one that Derrick never saw coming. When he originally planned to rescue her, he thought his involvement with her would be over within a matter of days. Now he realized how naive he had been. He hadn't considered all of the possible consequences, but bringing her home with him would have never crossed his mind.

Dixie barked and woke Larissa. "Is this it?" she asked with a yawn.

Derrick knew that his modest home on the lake was a far cry from the mansion Larissa was accustomed to, but the view of the water from his living room was breathtaking and should prove impressive to anyone. "I know this place isn't up to your standards, but hopefully you'll be comfortable until you decide where to go from here."

Larissa seemed barely awake as they walked into the side door. Derrick flipped on a light switch and said, "I'll show you around after we get some rest. We both need it."

He insisted that Larissa take the upstairs master bedroom. "No, that's not necessary," she argued. "I can sleep on the sofa. Actually, I could sleep on a rock," but Derrick insisted.

"You need your privacy," he said. "Now get on up there while I unload the car."

CHAPTER SEVENTEEN

Derrick awoke long before Larissa late that afternoon and nervously paced around the house. Not even Dixie could cheer him up when he stepped outside to give her fresh food and water. The smell of freshly brewed coffee, however, had an instant soothing effect.

Fortunately, the secluded location of the house offered almost total privacy. He rarely saw anyone around his property other than those in fishing boats at this time of year, but if Larissa happened to stay into the summer when owners returned to their seasonal homes, it could prove to be an ordeal.

The more Derrick thought about it, though, the more he realized that one advantage of having been an introvert was that he wasn't acquainted with anyone in the sparsely populated neighborhood. He'd always kept to himself, so no visitors would be stopping by unannounced to say hello. No one within miles knew what was normal at the Walton household, who should be there and who should not, so if someone happened to see Larissa from afar, her presence should arouse no suspicion.

Neither would anyone from church drop by unexpectedly. He hadn't attended services in over two years due to extenuating circumstances, but had maintained his faith through daily Bible readings, constant prayer, and watching services online.

How on earth would he explain Larissa's presence to Karen, though? His sister was a frequent visitor, and he couldn't very well hide his house guest every time Karen showed up. What would he tell her?

He listened intently for any upstairs movement, but apparently Larissa was still sound asleep, undoubtedly exhausted from the ordeal of the past several days. Derrick stepped into the kitchen for another cup of coffee but refrained at the last minute. Even the caffeine didn't settle his nerves. In fact, he'd never felt this skittish. His skin still tingled, though not as much, and he could almost feel his heart beating. The mounting stress of harboring a fugitive wouldn't help his declining health.

The only logical explanation, since he'd never mentioned another passenger when he'd spoken to Karen on the phone while traveling, was that he connected with Larissa somewhere during his final day of travel. What would sound believable, though? Why would a beautiful young woman, a cancer survivor for all appearances, take up with a complete stranger? Derrick had always considered himself to have been imaginative, but this story would certainly stretch those boundaries.

He would have had to have been approached by her when he stopped for gas or to eat. What could her story have been, though, and why would Derrick have been willing to bring her all the way home with him?

She had to have been running from something, in danger, with no one else to turn to. She wouldn't have been able to seek help from friends, relatives, or the police, but how could she have felt secure with an unknown traveler? The disguise as a cancer survivor would have had to have been her idea because she had to hide her identity from someone. She wouldn't have to maintain the ruse anymore, at least not around the house or the yard. Who could he say was after her, though, and why couldn't she go to the police?

Derrick hadn't even checked the local news, but he was certain that Larissa's story had made the headlines everywhere—here, too—so whatever scenario he made up couldn't mirror her actual situation too closely.

Could she be suffering from amnesia? Could she have begged him to take care of her until her memory returned? That sounded preposterous, like a Lifetime movie, but then again, so did the reality of the situation. Perhaps she had suffered a trauma of some kind. If they went with that story, Larissa would have to cling to him when Karen was around to show how frightened she was to leave his side. Would she feel comfortable doing that? Her behavior was entirely unpredictable.

Derrick shook his head and sighed. Karen was much too smart for that. Maybe Larissa could think of something better.

Finally, Derrick reclined on the sofa beneath a blanket watching the flames in the fireplace, enjoying the scent of burning hickory and the soothing crackles of the fire. It felt wonderful to be back home. As he grew drowsy, he heard movement in the upstairs bedroom. Within minutes Larissa slowly descended the stairs, pausing at the cedar rail to look down at him from upstairs with a blank expression. She still wore the loosely fitting polka-dotted dress from the day before.

"Are you okay?" Derrick asked.

She just stood there, silently staring. After a few moments he grew concerned. "Larissa?" he said.

It was then that he noticed tears streaming down both of her cheeks. Oddly enough, she hadn't cried when confronted by an armed intruder or when she was on the run and could have been captured any time they made a stop. If she had been caught, there would have been no bail; she would have been sent directly to jail as a flight risk. Now that she was in the safest place that she could possibly be, she was crying.

Larissa slowly eased down the remaining steps and padded into the living room to the sofa. Derrick got up, motioned for her to sit, and covered her with the blanket. She sobbed softly, and he hated to see her pretty face so red and puffy. At last she spoke.

"I'm here in a strange place where I don't belong, and I have no idea what to do next," she said. "I'm scared."

She began to shake, and Derrick felt compelled to wrap his arms around her shoulders. Fortunately, she didn't resist. She almost seemed to be falling apart, and a sudden panic struck Derrick. What if she needed health care? She had no health insurance, and she certainly couldn't give out her social security number. She would appear incredibly suspicious to any health care provider, who would undoubtedly report her to authorities, and that would be the end of it. Still, if her condition were serious enough, there would be no choice but to seek medical attention for her.

Thankfully, within moments, she began to calm down. "You don't have to do anything that you're not comfortable with," he said as he stroked the short, thick hair of her scalp. "You're not on any kind of timetable. Just take a deep breath. You're safe. No one will find you here."

"I don't care about that," she snapped. "I don't even know who I am anymore. I admit that I'm vain, but I don't know how not to be. And hiding from the world looking like this is like solitary confinement for me."

Ouch, that last comment stung. Did his presence mean so little to her that she felt like she was alone? Her vanity comment wasn't a flattering admission either, but Derrick understood. She had been a stripper, or showgirl, after all, accustomed to men gawking at her and massaging her ego. Now she was in hiding. The last thing she needed was someone recognizing her and associating her with the infamous girl on the run.

Larissa wiped her eyes and asked, "Is there anything to drink around here?"

Slowly shaking his head, Derrick answered, "If you mean alcohol, no; I'm not a drinker. But there's coffee."

Larissa groaned and collapsed against the back of the sofa.

"In fact, I don't have much of anything," he continued. "I'll need to run out for groceries sometime soon."

Pulling the blanket over her head, she cursed, and for the first time Derrick realized that having her in his home wouldn't be as easy as he'd imagined.

After Larissa regained her composure, Derrick gave her a tour of the house. They started at the door where they had entered on arrival. The house was a trilevel with the entrance located at the midsection. A cedar handrail lined the left side of the open hallway with the open living room visible at the lower level.

"This is an obviously empty bedroom," he said as he stepped along and motioned to the right. It was bare except for a couple of cheap framed reproductions on the walls. She made no comment as they stepped farther down the hallway. "And this is the luxurious bedroom where I slept last night," he joked as he pushed the door open. It looked about as drab as the other bedroom except for the full bed and night stand. A midsize flat screen TV on the wall that had wires hanging down looked almost out of place in such a dull room.

At the end of the hall to the left was a small bathroom, but prior to that were stairs going both up and down. "You know what it's like upstairs." She nodded. "And downstairs," he said as they descended four steps, "is the kitchen on the right and the living room to the left."

The creaking of the stairs as she stepped down grated her nerves. She was largely unimpressed and knew that her dour expression reflected her obvious discontent. Fortunately, the living room was the best part of the house. On the far wall a massive brick fireplace dominated the high-ceilinged room with bright orange flames and the smell of hickory. To the right, across the corner of the room, hung a large flat screen television. To the left of the fireplace stood a tall, dark antique armoire made of pine.

Two sofas sat catty-corner to each other, one newer and higher quality than the other. It was cream-colored with plush fabric, while the other was plain and basic with blends of burgundy and navy in the worn material, the likes of which probably occupied millions of homes. None of the living room furniture matched.

The place was modest at best, but she had to admit the view of the lake from the living room was stunning. The wall facing the lake was almost all glass. She stepped over to a ragged swiveling recliner facing outside. Yes, this million-dollar view deserved a more stately home than this. The cedar walls of the living room were far too rustic for her, and while the room was somewhat large by normal standards, she felt almost claustrophobic in such a confined space. Her three-car garage alone was as big as much of this entire house.

Only modestly decorated throughout, the house afforded a cozy ambiance, she had to admit, despite the thrift store decor. If it belonged to her, she would give it a complete makeover with hardwood floors and updated kitchen appliances. She decided, however, that the place was livable and kept reminding herself that at least she was safe at the moment. She could definitely relax here, and it was better than any prison cell, she supposed, but where would she go from here? At the moment she felt confused and lonely, every element of her previous life gone forever. It was akin to identity theft, only worse; her entire life had been stolen from her.

As the clouds dissipated and the sun shone brightly, Derrick called her to the front window to enjoy the view. It was indeed beautiful, but she was in no state of mind to actually "enjoy" anything.

"I need to run out to pick up some groceries," he said. "Will you be okay while I'm away? You can let Dixie come inside if you want."

"No . . . I mean, yes, I'll be okay, but I don't need Dixie. I need more rest, so I'll just lie down."

She settled on the sofa, and Derrick rekindled the fire. "Is there anything in particular you'd like me to get?" he asked. "Are you hungry for anything special?"

"No," she snapped. "Just go."

He did.

As he steered the Tahoe up the steep driveway, heavily wooded on both sides, Derrick noticed how strange it felt to be alone again in the car for the first time since this all began. It was also unusual leaving someone, a stranger, inside his home. No female other than his wife and sister had ever been in his house. He gripped the steering wheel tighter, his nerves still getting the best of him. The world seemed to be closing in on him, and at times it felt difficult to breathe.

He turned on the radio and listened to a local newscast. There was no mention of Larissa, but when he tuned to another station featuring national news, her story was indeed included, reported by a deep male voice:

"Fugitive or kidnap victim? No one knows for sure quite yet, say Arizona authorities regarding the disappearance of Larissa Baxter, who had been awaiting trial for the murder of her husband in Flagstaff.

"Harvey Bateman, Mrs. Baxter's attorney, made the following plea:

'To whomever abducted my client, please have compassion for her. She's been through enough already, and I fear for her.'

He paused briefly, then finished with, 'Larissa, if an opportunity arises, you know how to contact me. I'll personally come get you wherever you are.'

"Larissa Baxter is described as petite, five-foot-two, and a hundred and five pounds. She has long brown hair and blue eyes. If you see anyone matching this description who seems suspicious or out of place, please contact your local authorities immediately."

Derrick exhaled deeply. The state of affairs grew more real by the minute.

CHAPTER EIGHTEEN

After a couple of days at the lake house, tension had diminished somewhat. Having barely spoken to each other, Derrick and Larissa slowly shifted from cohabitation to actually getting along. Derrick sensed a lighter mood, and the two had actually shared a brief laugh or two. He tried not to overthink their circumstances and felt certain that Larissa had likewise decided to take things one day at a time instead of belaboring what appeared to be a rather hopeless situation.

She stepped into the living room still clad in one of the loosely fitting dresses he had bought for her at a Flagstaff thrift store and glanced at Derrick. The Eagles boomed over the stereo system, and Larissa nodded her approval, then said, "I need to do some laundry. I've already worn everything at least twice. Do you have something I can wear while my clothes are in the wash?"

"Hmm," he said, "a long-sleeve pullover shirt is about all that I can think of. I have sweat pants that would swallow you whole, so I don't think they would be an option. The shirt is long enough to cover you, though." She gave a non-committal shrug, so he assumed that meant she had no objection. He quickly went upstairs to retrieve one for her from his closet, feeling rising anxiety as he handed her the white long-sleeve Roll Tide shirt.

When she started upstairs she said, "I'll throw my clothes into the machine and take a shower. Then we need to talk."

Her tone sounded almost accusatory. Did she blame him for her circumstances? He realized more and more how poor his plan had actually been. Whisking her away from prosecution had gone well, but he had never considered how she might survive independently on her own. To that degree her predicament probably was his fault.

He heard the washing machine start filling and churning, then the upstairs shower came on. In a short while she came back down the stairs wearing only his thin, loosely fitting cotton shirt that, due to her petite size, dropped to just above her knees. Her short, scruffy dark hair, still damp and unruly, was wrapped in a towel. Nonetheless, she looked beautiful. He attributed her lack of discomfort at wearing only a thin shirt in front of him to the fact that she had been a showgirl and was accustomed to being around men only partially clothed.

Obviously she had a lot to say, but she seemed reluctant to speak. Instead of coming into the living room to sit, Larissa stepped to the window to gaze across the lake. Bright sunshine beamed inside, silhouetting her taut figure against the worn fabric of her shirt. Derrick saw the outline of every curve of her body, immediately struck by her physical perfection. He hadn't noticed another woman's beauty in years, but this was unavoidable. She was absolutely breathtaking yet seemed entirely unaware of the effect she had on him.

"The view from here really is amazing," she finally said.

The view from here ain't bad either, he thought, but wouldn't dare say it aloud. He promptly tried to steer his eyes and thoughts elsewhere. Viewing her from a sexual perspective would only complicate their situation. As she moved about the room, however, she was difficult to ignore. Larissa was one of the most striking women he'd ever seen, and she was right here in front of him. It was akin to having a top Hollywood starlet in his very own home.

How could he possibly think of anything else when faced with such a view of feminine perfection? He had always believed that God's greatest creation was the female form, ranking right alongside the wonders of the world. Could he vacation at the Grand Canyon and not look?

She was obviously nervous. "I'm curious about something," she began. "You've been away from work for a long time. Won't you need to go back soon?"

Surprised that she hadn't asked sooner, Derrick smiled and answered, "I'm self-employed—or was. I'm retired now."

She studied him hard, and he knew the wheels were turning inside her head. "You seem rather young for retirement. Most people these days don't retire until they're much older than you."

Those people don't know that their time clock is about to expire, he thought. "Well, I guess I'm the opposite of your husband," he admitted. "Material things don't matter to me. I've got everything I need, and I'd rather have time to myself than make more money."

Her expression was puzzling. Did she respect his choice, or did her desire for luxury cause her to see him as rather dull and boring? Regardless, the conversation had momentarily distracted him from her appearance.

Changing the subject, she asked, "What's next . . . for me?" as she relaxed in the recliner facing him on the sofa. "I feel like my identity has been stolen. I can't be myself. I've got to pretend to be someone else, and I'm not sure I can do that."

Derrick cleared his throat. "We've both got to make some major adjustments, and unfortunately, I don't have any answers."

She stared blankly at him, and the silence that hung in the air between them became maddening. Finally she said, "I have to admit, there were times when I wished he was dead. He hung out with some dangerous people."

"Your dad knew that," Derrick replied. "That's why he tried so desperately to convince you to leave him."

Larissa laughed. "Yeah, right," she said. "At the time I was still blinded by the good life and only heard what I wanted to hear. Besides, leaving the Baxter family isn't exactly easy to do. Marrying into them was the biggest mistake of my life."

Derrick nodded.

"I never understood how the Baxters maintained such a positive public image while there was so much darkness and hypocrisy in their private lives. I guess outsiders can be easily fooled."

"You know, Larissa," Derrick interjected, "we've all done things we've later regretted. You don't need to browbeat yourself. That's all behind you now, and you have a new life to live. Don't let your future be dictated by your past."

"Huh. Some life," she said. "Besides, wasn't it you who said you wanted to do something good with your life when you helped me? Wasn't that about making up for what you didn't do in the past?"

She had him there. Derrick tapped the screen of his iPad and changed the subject. "I found some websites that claim to offer legitimate-looking documents for the right price. Driver's licenses, birth certificates, social security cards—just about anything you could possibly need to reinvent yourself."

Larissa stood, and the silhouette of her body was again displayed against the bright sunlight outside. "I can't do it," she said. "I can't pass myself off as someone else. I'd rather be in jail."

She lifted her hands to stroke her drying hair. The washing machine finally stopped, and Larissa headed upstairs to put the wet clothes into the dryer.

Dixie barked outside, and Derrick stepped to the window to see what it was about. Two teenage boys ran across his lawn near the shoreline carrying fishing poles. Perhaps his house wasn't as isolated as he thought. He wanted Larissa to enjoy being outdoors, but she may need to be more discreet than he imagined.

Within minutes Larissa returned to the living room, still wearing the same shirt. Derrick couldn't help but stare. While she had her challenges, he obviously had his own. She sat in the recliner again and spoke as he returned to his spot on the sofa.

"This seems like a lonely place to me," she said, "but I never realized before how lonely my own life has actually been."

"How's that?" Derrick asked.

Larissa sighed. "Well, you cautioned me before about not trying to contact anyone I knew because they could be monitored by the FBI."

"Yes?"

"Well, the truth is, there actually isn't anyone I would want to get in touch with anyway. Isn't that sad?"

Derrick cleared his throat. "I'm not so sure how sad it is, but it's definitely surprising."

"What do you mean?"

"I thought you and your husband were socialites. I assumed you were with friends and at parties all the time."

Larissa laughed. "I lived in a plastic world. No one could possibly understand."

Silence hung in the air until Derrick eventually disclosed, "Loneliness is a state of mind. You can choose whether or not to be lonely."

Larissa laughed again. "Well, I don't have to worry about that anymore. I'll be lonely from here on out whether I like it or not."

A few days later Larissa approached Derrick. "I'm going crazy being stuck in this house, but I know you won't agree to me going shopping yet."

Derrick shrugged. "No, I don't think it would be the smartest thing to do. Maybe after the news story dies down it'll be okay." She was obviously frustrated, and he totally understood. "But, look, it's your call," he continued. "I don't want to control you in any way. It's your life, so you need to make the decisions."

She seemed to seriously contemplate the consequences, then said, "Well, I'm feeling more brave all the time, but I guess I'm okay with waiting a bit longer if you'll pick up some personal things for me."

After scribbling on a countertop note pad, she tore off a single sheet and handed it to him. Derrick scanned the itemized list, his eyebrows raised. "Whew!" he said. "I'll certainly attract attention carrying this female stuff to the checkout counter!"

She rolled her eyes. "Does that mean you won't do it?" she asked.

"Of course not! Nobody should suspect me of anything . . . unless someone who knows me sees me with these things. Someone who knows there isn't a woman in my life."

Shaking her head, Larissa quipped, "Then I'll have to do it. You can't expect me to live without the basics that a woman needs."

Derrick paused, in deep thought. "I suppose I could get Karen to—"

"There's no way!" Larissa interrupted. "She doesn't even know about me yet! And when you spring the news on her, she won't immediately buy into whatever we tell her and go shopping for me! That's insane!"

"You're right, you're right," Derrick acquiesced. "But suppose I wait until late tonight when I won't be as likely to be seen. Will that work for you?"

"Whatever!" Larissa dismissed him and stomped away in a huff.

Derrick gave a slight groan, realizing that having tiffs like this was one thing he didn't miss about having a woman around the house.

CHAPTER NINETEEN

B y the time Karen called ahead for a visit, Derrick and Larissa had their story straight, or at least it was the best they could come up with. How plausible it might sound was still in question.

As soon as Karen's car came to a stop in the driveway, Derrick took a deep breath and tried to calm himself before going outside to greet her and prepare her for what she would see inside the house. Karen's face beamed as Derrick met her beside her car with Dixie bouncing and barking at her side. He hadn't seen her since he'd left for Arizona. She quickly moved in for a bear hug and said, "Oh, it's so good to see you. Heavens to Betsey, you have no idea how much I've missed you."

Derrick gave her a kiss on the cheek and said, "Me, too. It seems like years instead of weeks."

As they walked toward the house Derrick prepared her with, "I've got someone inside I'm anxious for you to meet."

Karen shook her head and laughed. "Oh no," she said. "Not another stray! Derrick, I can understand you wanting one, but you absolutely don't need two."

Derrick chuckled inside and thought, *You won't think I should have what you'll actually find inside either.*

They walked along the upper interior of the house, then stepped down to the living room. Larissa sat on the sofa wearing one of her plain print dresses and a scarf. Derrick hoped she would stick to their ruse, make as little eye contact as possible, and give only short answers to questions.

As soon as Karen saw Larissa, she stopped in her tracks in obvious shock.

"Karen, I'd like you to meet Sarah," he said.

Larissa remained seated. She glanced up quickly, gave a half smile, then stared back at the floor. Karen seemed to be at a loss for words. "Well . . . Sarah . . . it's nice to meet you."

Derrick sat beside Larissa and motioned for Karen to sit in the recliner. "I have a crazy story to tell you, Sis, so please just listen."

"I can't wait," she said. Her suspicious expression told Derrick that this could be a harder sell than he'd imagined.

Larissa appeared fidgety, her hands in her lap rubbing her fingers together. She avoided eye contact with both himself and Karen. Derrick didn't know if it was part of her act or if she really was this nervous.

"Okay," Derrick began, "on my last day driving home I stopped at a rest area in Arkansas to walk Dixie. Sarah and her husband were at the same stop. He had been abusive throughout their marriage and had recently turned violent. When her husband was in the restroom, Sarah got into the back seat of my Tahoe and crouched in the floorboard while I was out of sight of the car. I didn't even know she was there until we were several miles down the highway."

"That's terrible," Karen said. "But why didn't you just take her to the police?"

"No!" Larissa interjected.

Derrick glanced at Larissa and slowly shook his head. "That's a good question. She won't explain why she won't go to the police. She just says she needs to stay hidden for a while for her own safety."

Larissa rose to her feet and started pacing around the room. *She's a good actor*, Derrick thought. *She really does look distraught.*

"But, Derrick, you can't just—"

"I know, I know," he interrupted. "She can't stay here forever, but I can't just kick her out either. She's in danger."

Larissa began to cry. Real or make believe, Derrick couldn't tell for sure. He returned to her side and soothingly said, "Hey, it's okay. Don't worry." He guided her toward the stairs and said, "Why don't you lie down for a while? You still need rest."

Larissa said nothing but slowly trudged up the stairs to the master bedroom.

When Derrick sat back down, Karen spoke in a whisper. "Well, I never would have expected *this* kind of stray." She hesitated as if contemplating what to say next. "Derrick, she's already been here with you way too long. You could end up in big trouble."

"I can't argue with you there," he said, "but I need to give her a little more time. Her husband has no idea where she is, so there's no danger of him kicking the door down. It'll all be okay in the long run."

"Is there more to this than meets the eye?"

"You mean something going on between us?"

Karen nodded. "Well, she's obviously sleeping in your bed!"

"Of course not!" He laughed, trying to make light of her suspicion. "I'm sleeping downstairs. Besides, how could you possibly think that someone who's young and looks like her could be interested in an old fart like me?"

"But—"

"Please, Sis, let's not talk about it anymore. I'm stressed enough about it already. Let's just catch up on things between the two of us."

Karen reluctantly complied, but the conversation remained strained. After almost an hour of awkward and virtually meaningless chitchat, Karen said that she needed to be going, so Derrick walked her to the door.

Before exiting, Karen paused and said, "Derrick, I don't like this. I can easily see it blowing up in your face."

Derrick hugged her and said, "Please don't worry. It'll all work out fine, I promise."

They said their goodbyes, and Derrick felt a sense of relief as he closed the door behind her.

It seemed to have gone better than expected.

Later that night Derrick checked the news in Flagstaff. A triple homicide had become the biggest local story, and no new developments about Larissa were listed on the television station's website, other than a possible sighting of her in El Paso, which made him grin. They had never been anywhere near that part of Texas.

Larissa had seemed rattled following her introduction to Karen, preferring to stay to herself in her room. Derrick wondered if she had truly bought into the concept of what still lay ahead.

CHAPTER TWENTY

D errick had already been away for a while to get the oil changed in the Tahoe. In the bathroom Larissa washed her hands and examined her stark reflection in the vanity mirror above the sink. Her blood froze at the sight of her closely cropped hair and face without makeup. It was eerie, almost as if a ghost of her former self was staring back at her.

Who am I? Why am I here?

A rush of heat flushed through her veins; her breath quickened. She began to erratically pace the hallway outside the bathroom door. *I can't do this anymore*, she thought. *It's too much for me. And I can't go back to Arizona without being sent to prison. I can't do anything. I'm stuck.*

Larissa swallowed hard, tears flooding both cheeks. "I can't . . . I can't . . ." she mumbled incoherently over and over. In Derrick's bedroom she searched his nightstand drawers and under his pillow for his handgun, knowing he hadn't disposed of it, but it was nowhere to be found. Rummaging through his medicine cabinet, she found nothing but an almost empty bottle of Tylenol, not nearly enough to put an end to her misery.

"I can't . . . I can't." Her mind swirling with deep dark thoughts, she hurried downstairs to the kitchen in a panic and retrieved a butcher knife from the wooden block on the countertop. It shook in her hand as she stared at its tip, imagining how easily it could slice through the tender flesh of her wrist. Next she rifled through the cluttered contents of a drawer for paper and pen, then remembered it was right there on the kitchen countertop all along. Feeling unsteady on her feet, she collapsed into a chair at the dining table, the knife on the tabletop to her left, the pen and paper to her right, her anxiety rising.

Now it became more difficult to breathe; she gasped for air. The sensation of heat she had felt earlier suddenly became a river of ice speeding through her veins. She stared blankly at the interior around her, the furniture, the cedar walls, the looming fireplace on the farthest wall. With knife in hand she gazed at her distorted image in the stainless steel blade like a funhouse mirror and turned the knife back and forth until sunlight through the window reflected a bright beam of light from the smooth metal surface, causing her to blink as she set the utensil back down to her left.

Tremors shook her right hand when she reached for the pen and slid the ruled pad of paper in front of her. Finally she took long, deep breaths to calm herself. Tears slid down her cheeks and dropped onto the paper. She had to stop her hand from shaking so she could write. After several more deep breaths, she thought the worst of the panic attack had passed. Now she could concentrate on the task before her.

Larissa closed her eyes, sniffled quietly, swallowed hard, then began to write.

> *Derrick, I can't do this anymore. I know you meant well, but it's just not right for me.*

She paused and sniffled again, wiping tears from her cheeks.

> *I appreciate all that you've done for me. I didn't deserve it.*

She stopped to gaze out the window at the wind blowing through the trees, creating ripples of waves across the lake.

> *But I have no future here or anywhere else, and this is my only way out.*

She paused briefly, then added, *I'm sorry*, signed her name across the bottom of the tear-stained page, and tore the single sheet from the pad of paper.

For how long she sat there in silence staring blankly ahead, she didn't know. Jarred from her mesmerized stance, she heard Dixie barking ferociously outside, scratching feverishly to get inside the sliding glass door from the deck just behind her. How could that mangy dog know what she was about to do? Dixie's howling echoed in her mind as she took the handwritten note from the table along with the knife, stood, and leaned her back against the sliding door, then slid all the way down to sit on the kitchen floor with Dixie still barking incessantly on the other side of the glass. With the note on the floor to her left and the knife to her right, she again stared blankly ahead, memories swirling in her mind.

When Derrick pulled to a stop in the driveway and exited the Tahoe, he immediately heard Dixie barking nonstop on the lake side of the house. Something was wrong. Hurriedly leaving the car, he rushed inside and called, "Larissa!"

There was no answer, although he heard loud sobs.

He dashed down the mid-level hallway, descended the four steps to the kitchen, and registered total shock at the sight of Larissa on the floor. As their eyes locked, Larissa quickly pulled a knife from her side and positioned its blade across the vulnerable veins of her left wrist.

Derrick froze. "No!" he shouted. "Larissa, don't!"

She sobbed uncontrollably, her pale face flowing with tears. Her lips quivered as she stuttered between sobs, "D-D-Don't stop me."

Torrents of dread coursed through Derrick's psyche. After all they had been through, it couldn't end this way. "Larissa, please!" he pleaded. "This isn't the way out!"

Dixie continued to bark relentlessly on the other side of the glass. Derrick watched Larissa press the blade closer against her flesh until a trickle of blood seeped through and dribbled onto her midsection. "Larissa, listen to me. This won't accomplish anything. You know I won't let you die. I'll call for EMTs and your cover will be blown. All of this will have been for nothing, and we'll both end up in jail."

She apparently tried to hold back tears but maintained her position. Fortunately, the stream of crimson increased only slightly.

Should I tell her that I'm dying, hoping that some semblance of sympathy within her might convince her to abandon her plan? For a moment he seriously considered doing so but then decided against it. She would survive this suicide attempt, and he didn't want to shift the serious nature of their circumstances away from her. His own plight couldn't overshadow hers. A sudden idea flashed through his mind as an alternate approach.

"Don't do this to your dad, Larissa." Derrick paused to watch for any sign that he was getting through to her as he slowly inched closer. "George set this whole thing in motion, don't you see? He's the one who saved you, not me. If he hadn't confided in me about his concern for you, I never would have come for you. Don't do this to him, Larissa—please! He's up there watching you," he continued, raising his head to the heavens. "Don't make him see this."

Her expression slowly changed. Hanging her head low, Larissa pulled the knife away from her wrist and dropped it. A slow stream of blood dripped from her wrist and formed tiny pools on the tile floor. Derrick rushed to her side, holding her tightly as tears ran from his eyes. "Please don't ever scare me like this again," he said between sobs. He pulled her closer and rested his chin atop her head. "Please . . ." he continued. "When you're feeling down and hopeless, talk to me. We'll get through this together, I promise."

He reached up and slid the door open for Dixie to come inside, her tail wagging now that the danger was over.

"Life is too precious to just squander it away," he said, "no matter how grave your situation might seem. God never gives us more than we're capable of handling. You'll get through this, I swear."

Even as he said these things, guilt overwhelmed him. Had he not himself done exactly what he cautioned her not to do? He had abandoned hope and refused treatment, giving up on his own existence. Life was indeed precious; even a diseased one.

Shaking himself back to reality, Derrick grasped Larissa's bleeding wrist and noted that it was only a minor cut. He helped her onto her feet, led her to the kitchen sink, and ran cold water over the cut as he ripped paper towels from the nearby rack to blot the wound until the bleeding stopped. He held her tight and locked eyes with her as she stared into his face, obviously noticing the tears streaming down his cheeks.

Derrick escorted her back to the sofa to lie down while he cleaned the blood from the floor. With dampened paper towels, he stooped to the stained tile and wiped away the blood, in the process spotting a single sheet of paper, a handwritten note. He reached for it, then paused. Did he really want to read this? What would it accomplish? He rubbed his forehead in deep thought, then wadded the paper and tossed it into the trash. Her written words would only upset him further, he knew, and he was an emotional wreck already, so he returned to Larissa's side on the sofa.

As her thoughts began to clear, Larissa felt the warmth of Derrick's embrace. His being so upset validated his concern for her, giving her strength and reassurance. He really did seem to see a light at the end of the tunnel for her, and that gave her a glimmer of hope. Her mouth opened and closed as she attempted to speak, but the words simply wouldn't come.

Despite her earlier feelings, something about her fate seemed more promising now.

A few days later, her suicide attempt now only a disturbing memory that they both chose to ignore, Derrick urged Larissa to leave the confinement of the house for the first time to enjoy a beautiful afternoon relaxing alone on the deck. Alabama weather had confused her. Only a few days earlier it had been brisk and cool, common for late October; today the temperature was in the mid-seventies. Derrick laughed and told her if she didn't like the weather to just wait a couple of hours and it would likely change; a bit of an exaggeration, but that was one of the things he liked about living here—there was always something different just around the corner.

It felt good to finally see her relaxing outside while he changed the battery in a bedroom smoke alarm. Suddenly he heard Larissa shriek, "Eww, get away, get away!"

In a panic he rushed outside to her and couldn't help but laugh at what he saw. Dixie had brought her a large dead fish and dropped it at her feet on the deck. Larissa was now scrambling back inside the kitchen, jumping on her tip-toes and screaming, "Take that thing away! Please!"

Derrick continued laughing. "It's just a fish!" he said.

"How did Dixie catch that thing?" she asked.

Her reaction was getting funnier, so Derrick laughed even harder. The levity of the situation was a welcome relief from when she had held a knife to her wrist. "She didn't catch it; somebody probably caught it and threw it back in, then it washed ashore."

"Why would someone catch a big fish, then throw it back in?" she asked.

Derrick finally calmed himself and tried to explain. "I don't know a lot about fish, but I do know that some are edible and some are not. That fish was probably one of the bad ones."

Larissa slowly shook her head. "You're a man of mystery, Derrick Walton," she said.

"How so?"

"Well, you know nothing about fish; in fact, you hate fishing, and you don't even own a boat, yet you live on a lake. What's wrong with that picture?"

Derrick smiled. "I've always loved water," he explained, then stepped aside and motioned out the window. "Some of my fondest memories are going to Gulf Shores with my folks and Karen. I'll never forget those days."

As Larissa calmed down, she said, "You haven't mentioned your parents. Are they still alive?"

Derrick hung his head. "They both passed away years ago. It's just Karen and me now."

"That's so sad," Larissa finally said. "I miss my dad terribly. But then there's my mom. She's still alive and well somewhere, I suppose, but there's no love lost between us."

Derrick squeezed her hand. "I'm sorry that you're not closer to her." Following an awkward pause, he continued, "But just look at this view. It's soothing enough to get your mind off almost anything. That's why I love it here. I don't need fish or boats to make me happy."

She nodded, then glanced down at the dead fish just outside the sliding door. "Hmm, I suppose so . . . but I want that smelly thing out of my sight!"

Derrick slid the door open, and the odor of dead fish overwhelmed them both. "Okay, okay, I'll take care of it."

Minutes later, after he had disposed of the rotting fish in the trash bin, Larissa stepped outside to join him on the deck. "Thanks," she said. "I appreci—ugh, the smell is still here!"

They sniffed around and realized the odor came from Dixie. "Okay, girl, you need to be hosed down," Derrick said with a grin.

Larissa joined Derrick at the side of the house with a bucket and a plastic container of dog shampoo. Together they giggled and washed Dixie for her first bath since she had come into Derrick's life. Dixie didn't seem to mind at all. As long as she was with one or both of them, she was apparently content.

Rinsing all the soap off Dixie, Larissa patted the dog's wet black head and said, "No more surprises for me, Dixie girl."

Derrick quietly shook his head. Their life together almost seemed normal. Who would suspect the bizarre events that had led them to this moment?

CHAPTER TWENTY-ONE

D errick felt an initial sense of relief when he checked the Flagstaff website and found that Larissa was still not a lead story. Yes, she was listed on the site, but was relegated to only a minor position in a list of "continuing stories." Derrick clicked *Baxter Manhunt Continues* and found no video, only text:

> There are no further developments in the search for accused murderer Larissa Baxter, who disappeared while awaiting trial for the execution-style death of her husband, Kenneth Baxter. She has not been seen nor heard from since. A nationwide search has thus far produced no valid leads.

Larissa's mug shot separated the text.

> If you see this person or have any knowledge of her whereabouts, please contact the Coconino County Sheriff's Office. A reward is available for information leading to her eventual capture.

Since there was no reference to Larissa as a kidnap victim, she was likely considered a full-fledged fugitive now.

A steady drip from the kitchen sink beckoned Derrick to come and twist the faucet handles tighter. He elected not to share this latest news with her.

***

One early November night Derrick led Larissa down the path to the pier guided by a low beamed flashlight. He carried a couple of quilts, and Larissa brought one as well. Dixie padded along beside them. After spreading two of the blankets to recline on, they lay flat on the padded surface and covered themselves for comfort with the remaining blanket. A brisk chill cooled the night air as they lay silently beside each other, each consumed with thoughts of their own. Derrick missed the endless drone of crickets and frogs from the summer months.

Dixie stepped to the very end of the pier and stared across the water, where the glimmering lights of a campground twinkled in the night on the opposite shore of the lake. Her curiosity abated, she padded back to her two favorite people in the world and lay at their feet on the worn planks.

Derrick inhaled the clean lakeside air and stared into the sky. So many stars were visible in this remote area of the state that it never failed to amaze him. A gentle wind churned the water into waves that lapped against the dock, and a buoy at the mouth of the cove clanged softly. He closed his eyes and thanked God for giving him such a wonderful place to live out his final days.

"You're quiet," Larissa finally broke the silence. "What are you thinking about?"

Derrick took another deep breath, then sighed. "I was just . . . thinking about my life . . . and everything that's brought me here."

She actually inched a bit closer. "You're a deep thinker, I've noticed."

"Mm-hmm," he answered.

"Is that how you decided to save me? Was it something you couldn't get off your mind, something you fixated on?"

"Something like that," he said, but offered no further explanation.

"But you still haven't explained why."

"Why what?"

"Why you put your whole life at risk for someone you didn't even know." She shivered slightly, then added, "I understand your connection with my dad, but there's still the possibility that you could end up in jail for an awfully long time."

Derrick cleared his throat, troubled by the direction this conversation was going. "It was the right thing to do."

Larissa turned to her side facing him, supporting herself on an elbow against the blankets. "Why are you being so evasive? Just tell me."

Derrick closed his eyes and rubbed his forehead with his right hand. Was this the time to tell her of his fate, admit that he felt a need to atone for the self-centered focus of his life? His breath quickened at the prospect. He didn't want to alarm her; not that he thought she would care, but because she might feel helpless and fear being left alone in the world.

"Well . . ."

Derrick swallowed hard but was saved by a meteorite soaring across the sky.

"Look at that!" he said.

Larissa raised up. "It's beautiful! It's like one quiet natural firework."

Dixie barked non-stop, obviously frightened by the mysterious light in the sky. Derrick took the opportunity to avoid Larissa's question and scooped up the blanket. "We should probably get back inside," he said, wondering when she might bring up the same topic again.

CHAPTER TWENTY-TWO

Two days later Derrick hurried from the deck when a smoke alarm blared from inside. As he pulled the sliding door open, clouds of smoke poured outside from the kitchen. "Larissa!" he called. "Are you okay?"

When the smoke dissipated, he saw her standing at the stove fanning flames rising from a skillet on one of the burners. Larissa coughed uncontrollably. He rushed inside, and after determining that the fire wasn't serious, dampened a nearby dish towel and tossed it over the flames to smother them, then ushered Larissa outside for some fresh air.

"Take some deep breaths," he urged her as they stood at the railing of the deck. When her coughs became few and far between, she could finally speak.

"I'm—uh—sorry," she apologized as she steadied herself against the rail.

"What were you doing in there?" Derrick asked.

"I wanted to surprise you with a home-cooked breakfast. I was scrambling eggs."

Derrick laughed and said, "Don't you think the burner was turned up too high?"

Recovering from one last cough, she answered, "Well, I . . . wasn't sure."

They sat at the picnic table, then Derrick went back inside to get a glass of water for her. Settling beside her, he tried to comfort her as she took a sip. "I appreciate the thought, but you didn't have to," he said.

Larissa gritted her teeth and stomped her foot. "Eww, I'm so mad at myself!" she seethed.

Placing a hand on her shoulder, Derrick asked, "Why on earth are you angry?"

She ran her fingers through her hair and confessed, "I don't know how I ever allowed myself to become so helpless."

Squeezing her shoulder, Derrick said, "How so?"

Facing away from him, she answered, "I've always been dependent. When there were people around to do things for me, I always let them. I never learned to cook, never did much house-cleaning; the only thing I ever did for myself was the laundry, when I lived in Vegas."

Derrick smiled and again tried to console her. "Well, it's never too late to learn. But you don't have to do anything to please me; I like you just the way you are. I would never judge you."

Larissa groaned, cursed to herself, then came back with, "You're so self-righteous. So you never judge anyone, huh?"

"Oh, so you're turning your anger against me now, are you?" he said in a calm voice. "That's okay. But, yes, I'm only human. I do judge people occasionally, but I'm not proud of it. God doesn't expect us to be perfect. He knows we're not capable."

Larissa quietly huffed at his side, apparently trying to calm herself. Suddenly she melted against him with an embrace, apologizing once again. "I'm sorry. I get so fidgety being cooped up in this house, and I shouldn't take it out on you."

Returning her embrace, he rested his chin on the top of her head and reassured her. "I totally get it. We've got to find a way for you to start living your life again."

As the Tahoe rolled to a stop in the dusty lot, Derrick noticed his sister's Toyota Camry parked a few cars down the row. She had arrived ahead of him.

The Shack did indeed look like a cabin, but the small rural restaurant served the best barbecue around. Karen had insisted that they meet alone; something was obviously troubling her. Could she and Roy be having problems again? Their marriage had been rocky from the start; for Karen, a second husband didn't seem to mesh with her much better than her first.

As he exited his vehicle, the scent of hickory smoke from the barbecue pit assaulted his nose, a smell he had dearly missed in Arizona.

Inside the aging rustic structure, Karen sat at a table in a far back corner away from other diners. She was already sipping an iced tea, and he tried to gauge her facial expression. She was obviously upset, but did it reflect worry or . . . anger? That didn't make any sense.

He smiled at her as he sat at the table, and she seemed to force one back at him. After giving the server their orders, Karen leaned across the table and said, "I'm so mad at you I could just scream!" He'd never heard such a harsh tone from her. Well, that eliminated Roy as her issue.

"What's this all about?" Derrick said.

Karen slumped back into her chair and exhaled. "Do you really think I'm that stupid, Derrick?" she whispered. "I don't feel like I even know you anymore. You've been like an entirely different person for the past few months."

"Well, I—"

"I know you went through hell with Sherry and all, but then you go running away to Arizona without explaining why and—"

Karen was interrupted as the server brought an iced tea to Derrick. He thanked her and glanced around the room. The hewn log walls were adorned with posters of racing legends from nearby Talladega Speedway and musical artists from the fifties. "Karen, I don't understand."

She rolled her eyes. "Derrick, I never bought that crazy story about Sarah for one minute." She paused for a deep breath. "You're a fanatic about locking your car when you stop somewhere, so there was no way she could have sneaked inside."

Derrick was flabbergasted and speechless. "It don't take a rocket scientist to figure out who she is," she continued.

"What . . . ?"

"You go to Arizona supposedly for as much as four months, then come home early with a young woman who's pretty as a peach at the same time that a gorgeous accused killer escapes from there on the run."

"Karen, you don't understand."

"She's all over the news. She can chop off her hair and wash off her makeup, but she can't hide that face. Did she seduce you, Derrick? Are you that weak? You're old enough to be her father!"

Now Derrick felt rising anger. "It's not like that, Karen. You don't understand."

"So it's true then? Gosh, Derrick, you're hiding a fugitive! You could go to prison! I can't believe this!"

As Derrick started to explain, he motioned for Karen to lower her voice as the server brought their food, a barbecue sandwich and fries for Derrick and a barbecue pork plate for Karen. As soon as the server was out of earshot, Derrick leaned closer to her and admitted, "I approached her, and it was my idea, not hers. There's nothing going on between us. She didn't manipulate me, and she's not a murderer."

Karen gave a fake laugh. "Yeah, right." She exhaled deeply and took a bite of her pork. "You're losing way too much weight, Derrick. Did you run marathons in the desert with her?"

They ate in silence, each avoiding eye contact. Laughter from tables in the next room seemed almost taunting as the tension ran deep between the siblings.

Finally, after finishing the last of his fries, Derrick ran his fingers through his thinning hair and expelled a burst of air. "Karen . . ." he said, then paused.

"Yes?"

"There's so much that you don't know."

"Goodness gracious, tell me about it! Are you losing your mind, Scooter?"

After refilling their iced teas, the server left their check on the table. Derrick grabbed it, and Karen didn't object. "I should be going," he said.

Karen placed her hands on her hips and said, "Do you mean you would just walk out and leave me hanging like this?"

Derrick slowly shook his head. "You can't imagine how much pressure I'm under now."

"Well, you're right about that. I can't believe the FBI is searching for my own flesh and blood!"

"Keep your voice down!" Derrick said in a loud whisper between gritted teeth. He massaged his forehead and said, "I have a terrible headache. I've got to go" as he stood from his chair.

"Derrick!"

He slowly sat back down. "Karen, please, just let it go for now," he said. "I have a serious health problem. That's why I went to Arizona, just to wrap my head around everything that I'll be facing soon."

"Then see a doctor instead of running away!"

He watched the blood drain from her face as she realized what he had said. He never meant to tell her this way, but he had to end this conversation, and it was the best way he knew to divert her attention away from the issue of Larissa.

"Derrick?" She reached out to him.

He held her and whispered into her ear, "It's not a simple fix, Sis."

Tears streamed down her cheeks, and she began to whimper. "No," she said with a moan. "You said it's serious?"

"We'll talk again later. I'm not feeling well, and I need some rest," he said as he threw a twenty and a five onto the table and turned to leave.

"Wait! You're not even going to tell me what's wrong with you?"

By the time he reached the door, she had caught up with him.

"Mercy, Derrick, don't do this to me!" she said. "Please tell me what's wrong!"

He hugged her again, then gently pushed her away. "I'll tell you more when the time is right, I promise." With that he pushed open the door and headed for his car. "I'm sorry, but I just can't talk about it right now."

As Thanksgiving approached, Derrick realized that Larissa never mentioned leaving anymore. Could it be that she was actually content living with him? It didn't seem plausible, yet there was no other explanation.

Karen had called him constantly, trying to pry information out of him about his health, but he adamantly refused to talk about it, especially not on the phone, for fear that Larissa might hear. "Please, just let me handle this as peacefully as I can," he had said to her. "I promise we'll talk about it soon."

Karen pushed him to plan for their traditional Thanksgiving dinner with her and her husband, Roy, and Derrick had a difficult time convincing her that it wasn't safe for Roy to know about Larissa, even under the false identity of "Sarah." Also, the one-hour drive from his lake home to Karen's place in Clay was problematic. What if they were involved in an accident and Larissa had no ID on her? No, he wasn't willing to take that kind of risk. Even with Larissa nagging him to go, he steadfastly refused. He knew she was probably going stir-crazy being confined to the house, but in his gut he felt that it simply wasn't worth the risk.

On a Tuesday night they sat watching television with a roaring fire in the fireplace. A blast of unseasonably cold air brought a light snow, and Derrick beckoned her to the window to see the faint dusting of white outside.

"It's pretty," she said. "I thought it never snowed here."

"Oh, it does occasionally," he answered, "but it's something us Southerners just never seem to get used to."

Derrick switched off the TV. Larissa returned to her comfortable spot beneath a blanket on the cream-colored sofa, and Derrick settled back into his recliner by the window. Larissa broke the silence by asking, "I notice that you're not into social media. You don't email, and I've never seen you text anyone."

Derrick smiled and slowly shook his head. "I've always been a telephone man for personal communication. I used email for business reasons, even had my own web page, but that's all the use I've ever had for the internet. What about you? I would imagine that most women around your age Facepage all the time."

Larissa laughed. "Facebook," she corrected him, "but no, I never got into it either."

"Why not?"

Larissa sighed. "I've had plenty of time to do a lot of thinking here." She paused momentarily, then said, "Remember when I complained about losing my identity when I first got here?"

"Of course."

"Well, I realize now that I lost my identity long before this. When I became Mrs. Kenneth Baxter, the old Larissa ceased to exist. I became this two-dimensional figure who pretended to be a socialite whose sole purpose was to improve my husband's image. My own needs were ignored. I guess that's why I never got into social media. I didn't know who I had become, and I didn't care to interact with anyone."

Derrick nodded. "I've wondered why you've never seemed interested in contacting anyone. Did you honestly not have a single soul you confided in?"

Larissa pulled the blanket up to her chin and winced at the sound of a sudden loud crackle from the fireplace. "Not anyone who mattered. Anyone who considered me a friend before has probably assumed I'm guilty. When I was arrested, nobody called; nobody cared. Who needs friends like that?"

That explained a lot. Derrick watched rather large snowflakes drift to the ground outside. If Larissa had nothing to go back to Arizona for, she probably was satisfied living in seclusion. It was hard to imagine, but she had apparently led a rather submissive life. At some point, though, she would have to move on; she seemed in denial about that.

Dixie scratched at the kitchen door to come inside, something that she rarely did. It was especially cold, however, so Derrick decided that she could stay in for the night. Sliding the door open for her, he smiled watching the big black dog prance across the living room to sprawl out on the floor in front of the fireplace.

A modest Thanksgiving meal at the Walton household consisted of precooked sliced turkey sandwiches, potato chips, and iced tea. Derrick had wanted to roast a turkey, but he'd never cooked one before, and recalling the earlier kitchen disaster with Larissa, he didn't want her near the stove again. He opted instead for a quick visit to the Publix deli.

The two of them sat at the small dining table squeezed between the living room and kitchen. Derrick reached out to take Larissa's hands across the table and said, "We need to give thanks."

She had a questioning look as she acquiesced, then bowed her head.

"Heavenly Father, we thank you for this food and the opportunity to honor you on this special day. You crossed our paths for purposes that we may not yet understand, and we ask you to safely guide us through whatever journey you have in mind for us. In Jesus's name we pray. Amen."

Momentary silence prevailed until after Larissa had taken the first bite of her sandwich. She said, "You haven't done that before."

"What? Give thanks?"

"Yes."

Derrick laughed. "But I should. I have a lot to be thankful for."

"You seem like a religious man, but I haven't seen a single Bible in this house. That doesn't compute."

Derrick laughed. "Well, you know, we do live in the twenty-first century. My Bible is on my iPad. I read it first thing every morning when I turn my tablet on."

Her face remained expressionless.

"You should try it sometime," he prodded her.

Larissa didn't respond. Instead, they shared a quiet dinner as holiday football played on the TV.

CHAPTER TWENTY-THREE

Days later Larissa stood at the kitchen door gazing across the water while enjoying a sandwich for lunch when she called Derrick to her side. "Look," she said, "is that man asleep in his boat?"

Joining her at the window, Derrick watched a small fishing boat powered by a trolling motor drift aimlessly in the waves about thirty yards from the dock. Inside sat an elderly African American man slumped over, his head almost between his knees, with a fishing rod at his feet, its line dangling into the water. "That doesn't look right at all," he said.

Derrick slid the door open, then stepped outside onto the deck. "Get my cell phone for me, please," he said. "Stay inside where no one will see you. If there's no way that I can handle it on my own, I'll yell for you."

"But do you think getting involved could expose us?" she reminded him.

"We may have to risk blowing our cover, but we can't let that man die."

Handing the phone to him, Larissa asked, "Are you really in good enough shape to help him?"

With a nod Derrick answered, "I'm strong enough to do something, even if it's only calling for help."

Standing at the edge of the dock, he called three times, "Sir, are you okay?" but got no response. Shrugging out of his clothes down to his underwear, he called nine one one, gave his address, then said, "I can't stay on the line. I've got to pull him to the shore so the EMTs can work on him immediately when they get here."

Dixie curiously trotted onto the pier and squatted beside Derrick's pile of clothes. He placed his cell phone on top of them, then sat on the edge to slide slowly into the water. The frigid temperature of the lake struck him like a pair of linebackers dousing him with icy Gatorade, but he tried not to think of it as he swam toward the man. The boat gradually drifted away, so he had to catch it quickly before he suffered hypothermia.

Almost halfway there, and oblivious to Dixie's leaping and barking on the pier excitedly, Derrick felt exhaustion and numbness setting in. *Got to keep going, got to keep going,* he told himself. Finally at the boat, he chattered in a loud whisper, "Sir . . . c-c-can you hear m-m-me?" Getting no response once again, he tried to reach inside to check for a pulse, but couldn't muster enough strength to pull himself over the side of the boat to touch the man. The realization struck him hard that it could be too late.

Determined to try every possibility to save the fisherman, Derrick grabbed the edge of the boat and kicked his feet hard to steer it toward the shore. The task would be easy, he knew, if it were summer and the water was warm. Under these conditions, however, it took every ounce of energy and willpower to guide the boat. Only ten feet from the shore, the water was still too deep to get a foothold, and he feared, even being this close, he may not make it. At least the arriving paramedics could treat him, too.

Inch by inch he continued to the shore, teeth rattling, finally mooring the boat to the muddy bank. Completely spent, Derrick crawled onto the grassy lawn and collapsed onto his back.

Larissa was frantic as she watched the events unfold from the warmth of the house. She stepped onto the deck for a clearer view and saw Derrick fall to the ground, breathing hard. Not hearing the sound of emergency vehicles, she was determined to get him back to the warmth of the house. She grabbed a blanket from each of the sofas and hurried barefoot down the gentle slope to Derrick's side.

Exposed to the cold now herself and feeling the growing pain on her feet from walking barefoot on pebbles, she covered him with the blanket, then did the same for the unconscious man. Derrick's eyes opened wide and he said, shivering uncontrollably, "Y-Y-You've got to get b-b-back inside before the E-E-EMTs get here."

Ignoring his request to hurry, she helped him to his feet and supported him for a slow walk up the slight incline to the house.

Once he was feeling warm and comfortable inside, Derrick asked, "How long has it been?"

Larissa wrapped the blanket around him tighter and responded, "About fifteen minutes or so."

Derrick groaned. "It takes the EMTs longer to reach this part of the lake. They've got to get here soon."

"So he's still alive?" she asked.

"I don't know. By the time I was in a position to check for a pulse, I collapsed."

At long last emergency sirens screamed in the distance. Derrick said a silent prayer that it wasn't too late.

Larissa stayed in her room upstairs to avoid any chance of detection as Derrick spoke to the paramedics outside. With sirens blasting, the ambulance eventually sped away, then she heard the sliding door close in the kitchen and raced down to meet Derrick.

"Is he—" she began, but was promptly interrupted.

"He has a pulse, but it's weak," Derrick answered, hanging his head. "It doesn't look good."

Giving him a long, hard hug, Larissa tried to console him. "You did everything you could even when you were in no condition yourself to do so. I'm proud of you."

***

Late that afternoon as Larissa sat on one sofa playing Sudoku and he on the other reading a magazine, Derrick heard a vehicle come to a stop in the driveway, followed immediately by low, guttural growls from Dixie that he'd never heard before. Obviously it wasn't Karen, whom Dixie would be happy to see, so it had to be a stranger, and that wasn't good.

He quickly rushed to the side door and peered out the peep hole. The distorted image revealed a commercial van of some kind parked in the driveway with Dixie crouched low, keeping its occupants at bay inside. He'd never suspected that Dixie would be such an effective guard dog, but then again, she had proven her protective nature time and again.

"Who is it?" Larissa asked from the living room.

"I've got to check it out to know for sure and keep them away from the house, but just to be safe, you should stay upstairs until I come back."

Outside on the wooden porch landing, Derrick saw that it was worse than he imagined. The vehicle was a mobile news van from an Anniston TV station, undoubtedly here to do a story on the rescue of the man in the boat. For someone who hated drawing attention to himself, especially with Larissa in the house, he had to find a graceful way out of this.

As he approached the van, he waved Dixie away. "It's okay, girl," he said, and the dog went scampering away to investigate something else.

When the van's occupants exited, he immediately recognized the attractive green-eyed reporter with red hair, Sally Mathers, but found her to be thinner than on TV. She pulled her thick overcoat tighter around herself and smiled despite the bitter cold. The cameraman, bundled in an overcoat that made him look like a purple Michelin Man, was otherwise nondescript—about as invisible in person as he was behind the camera.

After introducing themselves and shaking hands, the reporters explained that they would like to get some footage at the dock, then a few comments from him. With her breath sending frozen plumes into the air, Sally offered, "If it's too cold for you out here, we can shoot inside your house where it's more comfortable."

Not on your life, Derrick thought, recalling evidence of Larissa's presence scattered throughout the house, even in the living room.

"I'm sorry," Derrick explained, "but I'm far too camera shy for that. You're welcome to film around the pier all you want, but you'll have to leave me out of it."

Obviously disappointed, the reporter tried in vain to convince him otherwise, but he stood his ground. "Really," he responded, "it's been a traumatic day for me, and I don't want any fame or credit for helping that man. It was simply the right thing to do."

Reluctantly agreeing to his wishes, the two-person team thanked him for his time and stepped toward the pier.

Back inside the house, Derrick went upstairs to the master bedroom, still preferring that Larissa remain there until the news van pulled away, and filled her in on the visit.

The next morning Derrick stood in the living room as Larissa set a box of cereal and a container of milk on the table. Early morning condensation on the big windows limited the visibility of the beauty outside. Over breakfast Larissa took a sip of coffee and glanced across the table at Derrick. "I watched the ten o'clock news last night on that TV station after you went to bed," she began.

"And?"

"They did as promised and didn't even mention your name. They only referred to you as a 'good septarian' or something like that."

Derrick couldn't help but laugh. "I'm sure they must have said 'good Samaritan' instead."

"I've heard that term before; what does it mean?"

Not wanting to get into another biblical discussion so soon after the prayer talk for fear that too much religion too soon might turn her off, he answered, "I'll explain later." He'd been around well-intentioned people before who wore their Christianity on their sleeves and pushed too hard to win people over to the Lord. He had a strong opinion that that wasn't the most effective way to introduce spiritual life to an unbeliever, and he didn't dare take that approach with Larissa.

"Anyway," she continued, "the man is in intensive care with a fifty-fifty chance of survival, but I was irritated by the fact that in a clip of his family, the man's wife gave God all of the credit instead of you."

Derrick pursed his lips and slowly shook his head. Now may not be the right time, but he would eventually need to find an opportunity to discuss coincidence versus divine intervention with her. Of course God deserved all of the credit. It wasn't at all by mere chance that the man just happened to have a heart attack within view of the only people living on this section of the lake at this time of the year. God hadn't caused the heart attack, but He had placed the man in a position where he would likely get immediate help; however, he still didn't want to overload Larissa with another pious discussion so soon.

"You'll be pleased to know, though," Larissa interjected, "that Dixie made her first television appearance. She was jumping all over the pier in the background."

Derrick couldn't help but smile. How he loved that dog.

CHAPTER TWENTY-FOUR

An icy mood had hung over the house until finally, a few days later, Larissa settled on the sofa with Derrick's iPad. The latest news from Flagstaff was disturbing. "Derrick, come and look at this," she called to him. He came immediately.

It wasn't a major story by any means and was relegated to only a brief article: *Baxters Offer Million Dollar Reward.*

The two read it together:

> Flagstaff, AZ—A spokesperson for the family of slain businessman Kenneth Baxter states that the victim's family has offered a one million dollar reward for information leading to the capture and conviction of accused killer Larissa Baxter, who remains at large. Previous reported sightings in Reno, Nevada and Boulder, Colorado have proven unsubstantiated.

Once again, Larissa's mug shot separated the text.

> Any sightings of Larissa Baxter should be reported immediately to your local sheriff's office.

Derrick scratched his head. "What's your take on that?" he asked.

"Well," Larissa began, "it's a big attention-getter, but they would never pay out that kind of reward. They would find some loophole to get out of it. That's just the way they operate."

The clatter of ice into the tray, then the hiss and thump of the refrigerator's automatic ice maker filling broke the momentary silence. Derrick deeply exhaled and slowly shook his head. "Yeah, but nobody else knows that," he finally said. "Every bounty hunter and kook in America will be desperately looking for you now to hit the jackpot. It complicates our situation even more."

"*Our* situation?" she asked.

Derrick rolled his eyes. "In case you haven't noticed, we're in this together."

Larissa stood and stepped into the kitchen for a glass of water. "You know," she said, "this might sound crazy, but I'm growing less concerned. I do feel safe. Who could possibly look for me here?"

Derrick gazed through the big front window, across the water. In addition to the smell of burning firewood from his own fireplace, he noticed wisps of smoke rising from the chimney of another waterfront home about a half mile farther up the shoreline along the bend of the cove. "We need to be more aware of fishermen. This is one of the hottest spots on the lake. You've seen how guys will sit in their fishing boats right alongside the dock, sometimes for hours at a time. It's far enough away from the house that I don't think they could see you, but if you ever notice one with binoculars looking this way, let me know immediately."

Even Larissa herself didn't understand her new calm demeanor as Derrick stepped over to stoke the fire.

In early December it dawned on Derrick that the regular college football season was over, and for the first time in his adult life he hadn't been interested in the SEC standings. He'd seen the Crimson Tide scores from time to time online and knew they were having another good year, but his thoughts had been entirely focused on Larissa's plight and his own failing health.

He had begun to visibly decline and had to admit disappointment that Larissa hadn't seemed to notice. His hair continued to thin as he watched body hair swirl down the shower drain. Inside, it was much worse. He felt weak, and his body ached in places that it never had before. His health aside, at least Larissa seemed content, but how was she staying so lighthearted? How could she not be missing her former life? Derrick had grown up in a tight-knit, loving Southern family and couldn't imagine how Larissa had been raised. Her dad had been a great man but had a hard edge to him because of his 24/7 focus on murder investigations. Larissa had suffered as a result.

Derrick stepped outside onto the deck to feed Dixie and felt his energy draining. Sitting on the picnic table bench to watch the dog engorge herself, he wondered what his life would be like as his health further declined. How would it impact Larissa?

He was far more concerned about her than himself.

CHAPTER TWENTY-FIVE

As Derrick prepared to leave to meet Karen again, Larissa exercised in the living room, dressed in her provocative workout gear from the night he confronted her. He watched her bend and stretch, noting the firmness of her body but also realizing that his attraction to her had diminished. Sadly, it had to be yet another symptom of his declining health; his libido was now almost nonexistent. For Derrick, it felt like the beginning of the end.

He called down to her, "Bye. See you later."

Larissa looked up with a smile and answered, "Be careful."

The Pell City Steak House was only thirty minutes from Derrick's home. As he drove there to meet Karen, he still felt guilty for having kept his health a secret from her for so long. From the beginning he had questioned his decision to refuse treatment and keep Karen in the dark, but at this point it was too late. Nausea taunted him most days now, no matter what he ate.

He knew Karen was terribly upset, both at him and for him, and there was no excuse for ignoring her calls and having been so evasive with his only remaining family member. She had no idea what he'd been living through, but that didn't matter; he should have been more considerate of her feelings.

As usual, when he pulled into the restaurant parking lot he saw Karen's Camry already there. As he exited his car and slammed the door, he noticed from the corner of his eye Karen doing the same. She wasn't waiting for him inside as she typically did; instead, she raced toward him, arms open wide and tears streaming down her cheeks.

They embraced without a word, hugging each other tightly. Karen seemed to be having trouble regaining her composure.

"It'll be okay," he whispered softly into her ear. He felt her hold lighten and had to grasp her to keep her from falling. "Are you alright?" he said.

"How could I be alright?" she answered between sobs. "You and Roy are all I've got left, and I sometimes have my doubts about him."

He helped her steady herself and started to guide her toward the restaurant door when she stopped him. "Hold your horses," she said. "We can't have this conversation in there. Let's sit in my car."

She was right, he knew. The weather was cool, so it would be comfortable inside her car, and this talk would be far too emotional and personal to be done in public. He helped her back to her Camry and eased her into the driver's seat, then settled into the passenger seat beside her.

"I'm sorry that I've done this to you," he began, hanging his head. "I thought my life had bottomed out after I lost Sherry, then it wasn't long after that until I got the news from my doctor. I haven't been myself since, but that's no excuse for not considering your feelings. I truly am sorry."

"It's okay, it's okay," she said. "What's important is what's going on now. What can I do to help? You don't have cancer, do you?"

It was a natural assumption since both of their parents had been victims of the disease, but that wasn't it. Derrick massaged his forehead and faced away from her. How could he even begin? She wouldn't like what he had to say, but he would stand his ground. There had been few moments in his life as difficult as this. His eyes moist with welling tears, he finally faced her. "I've decided not to tell anyone what it is," he said.

Her face showed surprise and confusion. "What?" she responded. "Why on earth would you do that?"

Derrick cleared his throat and watched an elderly couple enter the restaurant. He would be long gone before he could ever advance to that age. He took a deep breath, then slowly exhaled. "Karen . . ." he started. "Please try to understand, and don't fight me on this." A lone train whistle approached from a distance, and he glanced toward the nearby tracks. "I don't want anyone Googling treatment options and giving me advice. In fact, I don't want to talk about it at all. I want to live every last day as normally as possible. God has decided that it's my time to go, and I don't want to interfere."

Karen slumped against the driver's seat. "*What?*" she exclaimed. "Please, Derrick, don't tell me it's that bad!"

"Please," Derrick interrupted her, "if you want me to go in peace, just let me do this my way."

"But I can't help you if you don't—"

"You can't help me anyway," he interjected again. "No one can." He paused and swallowed hard. "When I first got the news, I never would've thought that my final days would play out this way. I have Larissa to think about and—"

Now it was Karen's turn to interrupt. "Has she been playing tricks with your mind, Scooter? Is she behind this?" He shrugged. "I've been doing some research on her. She was a gold digger when she married that shady husband of hers. Is she trying to get her hands on your money now?"

Derrick's anger showed clearly in his expression. "Don't say that!" he said tersely. "She's not that way at all. You shouldn't assume things like that about people you don't even know."

Karen took Derrick's hand in hers, and following a brief pause asked, "Do you love her, Derrick?"

The question caught him completely off guard. The thought hadn't crossed his mind, yet he had to admit there was an uncanny bond between the two fugitives. Yes, it was definitely love from his perspective. It wasn't the romantic kind, but only because he had tried so hard to suppress his emotions. Larissa couldn't possibly feel the same. She was so far out of his league that it was pointless to even think about it.

Regardless, it felt good to admit to himself that he was in love with her. He looked Karen in the eye as she waited for an answer. Glancing down, he said, "Well . . . I can't say that I'm not in love with her."

He watched Karen grip the steering wheel, and she seemed to grit her teeth before she finally scolded, "Derrick! How can you let someone like that twist you around her little finger?"

He grew more and more uncomfortable, ready for this conversation to end. Summoning all the assertiveness that he could muster, he said, "Look, I've already told you that she doesn't try to manipulate me. It's all my decision."

"And what if—"

"Karen, I need to leave. Just accept that my final wishes are what's best for me and her. I want to live without thinking about dying, and I want my time to be with her. I can't explain it, and you'll never understand it if you try, so just let it go." He reached for the door handle and started to exit the car.

A final thought struck Derrick before leaving. "I don't want to make this about me," he began. "Knowing that my life is almost over has changed me. I've realized even more how inconsiderate I've been my whole life, how I've been focused on everything but the right—"

"Hush your mouth," she scolded him. "That's not true. You've always been the kindest, most compassionate man I've ever known, and I don't want to hear you say otherwise."

Derrick sobbed, but managed to say, "But you don't know me as well as you think you do. We never know others like we think we do. It's impossible."

"But what good does it do to punish yourself? The only thing that matters is what happens from this point forward."

"That's right, but—"

"You've always been a strong man of faith, Derrick. Do you honestly think people reach this point in their life without making mistakes along the way, without having regrets?"

"Yes, I know what you're saying. I've said the same thing to Larissa."

"So if God forgives you, why can't you forgive yourself?"

Derrick hung his head and remained silent as he pulled the door handle and opened the door slightly. "Larissa doesn't know that I'm sick," he said. "Not that it will matter to her anyway, but please don't say anything to her about this. I'll tell her when the time is right."

"Ah," Karen said, nodding and reaching for his hand, pulling him closer. "That's what the whole Larissa thing is about, too. You're wanting to do something good for someone else to make up for your past indifference, and she just happens to be a beautiful stripper."

Derrick felt his anger surge again. "Stop it! Everyone has a past," he said, then squeezed her hand. "Larissa is the daughter of a good friend, one of the best friends I've ever had, in fact. I never should've let that friendship go away. That's another mistake that I regret."

"Derrick, please stop it," she interrupted. "I don't want to hear anymore of that. You're so wrong. I've never seen a more devoted husband than you. There's nothing in your past that you have to make up for. You've just got to focus on getting better."

Derrick realized that he couldn't end the conversation like this. He pulled the door shut, turned toward her, and slowly shook his head. "That's not going to happen," he said. "I refused treatment."

"You *what?*" she responded in obvious shock. "How could you do such a thing? It's probably not too late to—"

"Yes, it probably is," he said, "but that's okay. I'm at peace about dying. I'm probably more at peace about dying than I am about living."

Karen pounded the steering wheel in obvious frustration, her sobs returning louder this time. "DERRICK, PLEASE!" she screamed. "You can't be dying!"

Derrick hung his head and didn't respond. "My gosh, Derrick—how much time do you have left?"

His arm around her, he patted his sister's knee. She was the one person who had remained by his side throughout his life. "What does it matter at this point?" His voice had a wheezing sound as he became more upset. "Best case scenario, maybe six months, I would guess," he said. "The way I've been feeling lately, probably no more than a few weeks at most."

Karen turned to him and held him tightly, her sobs changing into moans, her grief growing more uncontrollable by the moment. He hated seeing her this way. She was a nervous wreck. He should have handled this better.

"My world is spinning out of control," she managed to say between sobs.

Holding her tightly and lovingly patting her on the back, he whispered, "You're the best sister any man ever had. You've always believed in me. You've always had my back."

Tears streamed from his own eyes now. "Thank you for always being there," he said. "I've never thanked you before."

After several minutes of silently holding and consoling each other and weeping together, he felt comfortable leaving her, confident that she had enough control of herself to drive home safely. Stepping back to his car, he came face-to-face with a cop heading toward the restaurant door and almost froze in place. He didn't like fearing the police—he never had—but just couldn't help himself.

Teardrops blurred Derrick's vision as he steered the Tahoe back home wondering what he would have done without Karen in his life.

CHAPTER TWENTY-SIX

"**D**errick, you've never mentioned children. I assume you've never had any?"

It was another night with the fireplace blazing. No lights were on, and the flames cast dancing shadows across the walls. The smell of the hickory and crackle of the fire created the perfect ambiance. The forced air furnace kicked on—the home's primary source of heat—blowing warm air through the floor vents. For any other couple it would have been romantic, but the two sat warm and comfortable beneath a blanket together on the sofa facing the fireplace, barely touching.

A sorrowful expression spread across his face. "No," he said. "We wanted children, but Sherry couldn't get pregnant. I would've loved to have a kid or two."

They locked eyes, and Derrick smiled weakly. "What about you?"

"Yeah," she said, "what about me." She seemed to carefully consider what she was about to say. "Ken was adamant about not wanting kids. He was one of the most self-centered men I've ever known."

"But you?"

"I didn't fight him about it." Larissa paused, apparently deep in thought. "I grew up as an only child and a cop's kid. It wasn't a very nurturing environment. I guess I didn't have much of a motherly instinct, so I just let it go. Besides, I couldn't in good conscience bring a child into the world with Ken as its father."

Derrick nodded. "It's sad to say, but it doesn't sound like a functional marriage."

Larissa groaned. "It's hard to even call it a marriage."

Derrick continued to nod.

"But yours was good?" she asked.

Derrick made a pitiful smile. "I thought so, but apparently it wasn't." He sighed. "I guess I've always had a tendency to see the world through rose-colored glasses. I didn't recognize what was right before my eyes, and I ultimately paid the price."

Larissa stretched her legs and yawned. "We're both a couple of Debbie Downers. I think I'm ready to call it a night."

Derrick yawned as he rose from the sofa. "I'm exhausted," he said, his muscles aching all over. "I'll be asleep before you make it upstairs."

Karen made a surprise visit to Derrick's home several days later. As she pulled the Camry to a stop in the driveway, Dixie came bounding around the corner of the house barking and leaping, obviously happy to welcome a guest.

Karen wasn't quite sure how this would go. She obviously had to accept Larissa for Derrick's sake, and hopefully she could keep her contempt for the woman under control.

As she stepped onto the small cedar porch, Derrick opened the door with a look on his face that was virtually unreadable. Was he angry about her unexpected presence or just surprised that she had come unannounced? It was almost as if she didn't know her own brother anymore, and it didn't really matter anyway. She was worried sick about his health, and aside from that, she had to get a few things off her chest.

"Well, look who's here," Derrick greeted her. Did she note a hint of sarcasm in his voice, or was she perhaps reading too much into her brother's reaction?

"Hi, baby brother," she said as she leaned in for a big hug. "Did I catch you at a bad time?"

"No, not at all," Derrick answered as he stepped aside for her . to enter.

Pacing down the hallway, Karen felt relief that Derrick seemed normal and in a good mood. Larissa sat on one of the sofas below in the living room, looking up at her. Her earlier resolve abandoned, Karen couldn't help but take a dig at the fugitive as she made her way to the sofa adjacent to Derrick's unusual guest. "Well, hello, Sarah . . . Larissa . . . or is it something else today?"

Larissa's face showed a hint of embarrassment knowing that Karen was aware of her true identity, but not expecting her to launch a verbal attack. She opened her mouth to speak, then said nothing, instead looking down and away from Karen. Derrick settled beside Karen on the sofa, and with his arm around his sister, he reprimanded her. "Now there's no call for that. If you're going to harass Larissa, you might as well—"

"You're right," she agreed, then turned to Larissa. "I apologize," she said. "I promised myself before I got here that I wouldn't disrespect you, but it just slipped out. I truly am sorry."

Larissa didn't speak, still visibly upset and instilling painful guilt in Karen, who then sat beside Larissa to comfort her. During an uncomfortable silence, a falling pine cone thumped against the roof of the house as if to break the ice between the three. Placing an arm around Larissa's now quivering body, Karen hugged her tightly and said, "Please forgive me. I know how much you mean to my brother, and his friends have always been my friends."

Slowly Larissa seemed to regain her composure; a weak smile appeared. She meekly looked Karen in the eye and said, "It's okay. That was far from the worst that I've experienced lately."

Karen gently patted Larissa on the knee, then sternly faced her brother. "But you, Scooter, I expect some clarification from that bombshell you dropped on me at—"

"Hold on!" Derrick interrupted, continuing as he motioned with his eyes toward Larissa. "This is neither the time nor place for that."

Immediately recalling that Derrick had not yet told Larissa about his illness, Karen backed off. "Yes, this may not be the place or time, but we have a lot to discuss someday," she said with a tone of sarcasm. "My purpose for coming today was to speak with Larissa more than you anyway."

Derrick laughed. "Well, I can certainly take a hint," he said as he got up from the sofa and stepped into the kitchen and out onto the deck. "I'll just excuse myself and let you two get to know each other better."

Knowing that Larissa was probably not interested in getting acquainted, Karen realized that she must proceed cautiously. As the glass door slid shut with Derrick outside, she faced Larissa directly and forced a smile. "Well . . ." she began, "I don't mean to intrude or cause you any discomfort, but my brother means a lot to me. I've always been a protective big sister, and Derrick has been through so much lately that I can't help but look out for him."

A semblance of a smile broke free from Larissa as she began to seem more receptive. "He speaks so well of you," she said. "I never realized how much I've lost in life by not having a sibling."

An awkward silence chilled the air until Karen nervously began to pry. "Larissa . . . I . . . Well, Derrick is so vulnerable now and—I wish I hadn't started us off on such a bad note earlier, but there's no delicate way to say this . . . I just need some reassurance that you're not taking advantage of my brother."

For some reason Larissa seemed dumbfounded. "You think— now wait a minute. I don't know what he's told you, but this was all his idea. He had to convince me to leave with him. In fact, he almost begged. At the time I was totally vulnerable and didn't know what to do."

Karen nodded. "Yes, that's essentially what he told me," she said.

Larissa sighed, then looked Karen directly in the eye. "You have no idea what I've been through, starting with my husband's death." She paused and took a deep breath. "And then, along comes your brother. Can you even imagine what it's like to be confronted by a masked man with a gun inside your own home?"

Now Karen was taken aback. "*What?*" she questioned. "You're not saying that Derrick—"

"That's exactly what I'm saying," Larissa said.

Karen shook her head. "Mercy, darlin', I wasn't born yesterday. You'll never convince me that Derrick actually did something like that. He's a lot more lamb than lion." Her expression was stern, almost unforgiving.

Pursing her lips, Larissa slowly nodded and blurted, "He said it was totally out of character for him, and he didn't know for sure what came over him. Ask him yourself."

Karen sat stunned and speechless. How could something like that even be possible for a man who had always been so meek?

"So you're saying he held a gun on you until you agreed to leave with him?"

"Yes—no, he didn't hold the gun on me. In fact, he gave the gun to me to prove that he wasn't forcing me to do anything."

Karen was stunned. This sounded preposterous, but could it actually be a side of Derrick's personality that she had never seen?

"I told him in the beginning that I didn't want to come to Alabama, and he was okay with that," Larissa continued. "And when I later changed my mind and really did want to come home with him, he was okay with that, too." Larissa paused, glanced down at the floor, then raised her head to look back at Karen. "He's been in control the whole time. I never tried to influence or take advantage of him at all."

This last comment raised Karen's ire. She tried to maintain her composure, then snapped, "Now, wait a minute. He's been in control? Are you accusing my little brother of holding you against your will?"

Larissa laughed. "Absolutely not!" It took a moment for her to recover from the accusation. "Derrick? Controlling? Not on your life! He never coerced me to do anything. His whole purpose in rescuing me was to give me freedom, not to be possessive, and that's exactly what he's done."

Outside the kitchen door, Dixie's claws and pads scraped against the surface of the deck as she scurried around playing with Derrick. Inside, Karen wasn't sure that she was buying Larissa's story. She leaned forward and whispered assertively, "Can you honestly look me in the eye and tell me that you didn't kill your husband?"

Shaking her head, Larissa stared back at her. "You don't know me, and I totally understand that you have your doubts. I know that I *look* guilty, but no, I did *not* kill my husband. I wanted out of the marriage, but not that way."

"So then why aren't you somewhere else starting this new life you're talking about? Why are you still here?" The whole thing still seemed far-fetched.

Larissa leaned against the back of the sofa and glared. "Karen, I know you mean well, but I don't appreciate being interrogated. This is actually none of your concern. Your brother is a grown man, and he's doing what he wants to do. This is his mission, not mine. Just ask him."

Karen ran her fingers through her hair and exhaled a deep breath of air. "Then help me understand this hold you have on him. I agree, it's not my business, but is there something else going on that would help explain this whole thing?"

Larissa spoke through clenched teeth, "This conversation is going nowhere. You need to talk to Derrick, not me."

Karen shrugged, stood, and turned to go outside to confront Derrick. "Just remember," Larissa cautioned, "the more you dig at him, the more you'll be alienating yourself from him. You don't really want that, do you?"

Stopping before she reached the door, Karen realized that Larissa was right. She couldn't risk distancing herself from Derrick when he was possibly living out his final days. To the contrary, she had to make amends with Larissa and be on her way.

Larissa stepped toward her, and Karen, teary-eyed, held out her arms. "I'm so sorry," she apologized. "I truly am. Goodness gracious, I came here with good intentions, and I've done nothing but alienate us further. I want what's best for my brother . . . and for you, too."

They hugged longer than was actually necessary, and when Karen broke away, she continued, "Someday I'd love to hear the real story between you two; not from being nosey, but only because I care." With a broad smile she finished with, "I have a feeling that you and I will be growing much closer in the not-too-distant future."

"I hope so," Larissa said. "Derrick whisked me away because he felt that I was in dire need, but he's still so broken up over his divorce that I'm convinced he has needs of his own that I don't know about, maybe even more than mine. Hopefully, together, you and I can make him happy again."

Exhaling deeply, Karen stood silently with a blank expression that turned questioning. Larissa glanced at Derrick through the window, then said, "He's such a private man. He never talks about himself. What made his divorce more difficult than usual?"

Expelling a burst of pent-up air and slowly backing away, Karen paused, then finally said, "I don't mean to be rude, but I honestly think you need to hear that directly from him. He's sensitive about it and would be upset if he knew that I told you anything."

With a weak smile, Karen stepped outside and found Derrick sitting on a deck chair facing the water. He tilted his head to look up at her as she patted him on the shoulder with her left hand, then sat at the picnic table to his right. "Alright, Scooter, let's talk," she said.

Derrick glanced back through the window, apparently to see how close Larissa was, then answered, "Okay, as long as you keep it down. Larissa's got enough on her plate to add concern about me."

Tears blurred and distorted Derrick's image before her. Karen almost felt her heart sink when she recalled his words from before. "We've always been honest with each other," she said. "I haven't quite forgiven you for leaving me hanging like you did the other day."

"Look, Sis, I apologize for that," Derrick said, "but I just can't give you any specific details. Caring for Larissa helps me cope with my own problems. I'm feeling pretty good today, but it can change from one moment to the next."

Karen slowly shook her head. "I can't understand how she could be so important to you when you hardly know her. What makes you so devoted to her?"

Pausing to rub his forehead with his fingertips, Derrick finally replied, "I honestly didn't expect it to turn out this way. I never dreamed she would come home with me or that I would have feelings for her. I can't explain how much better I feel about myself just taking care of her. She's making my final days so much better, so please don't try to interfere."

Now Karen spoke in a whisper as if eavesdroppers were present. "Despite all of that, how can you be so comfortable spending your final days harboring a fugitive, always watching your back?"

Derrick hung his head. "I guess I can't really expect you to understand." He reached out for her hand and squeezed it tightly. "I love you, Sis. You know that. And besides, she may be a fugitive, but she's *not* a murderer." He leaned in for a hug, then implored, "If you love me, you'll let me see this through. Maybe Larissa will start a new life somewhere else before my time is up. If not, I hope she'll be with me until . . . the end."

Karen felt more confused than when she first arrived, but she couldn't take anymore. Her mind was spinning, and she knew that staying any longer wouldn't accomplish anything. Rising to her feet, she leaned over to hug her brother again, but he stood to embrace her, and they shared perhaps the longest bear hug of their entire lives. Sniffles choked her, and she cleared her throat. "Please stay in touch. Don't ignore me anymore."

"I would never ignore you," he answered as Karen pulled away and stepped down the deck stairs to walk across the lawn to her car.

She had never felt so empty.

CHAPTER TWENTY-SEVEN

Bright sunlight glistened across whitecaps kicked up by a heavier than usual wind across the lake. Derrick never tired of the gorgeous view from his living room, but he wondered what Larissa really thought about it. She'd been accustomed to far more luxurious accommodations and exotic locations, but he wouldn't trade his little spot on the planet for anywhere else. This was home, and with time running out in his life, it was the perfect place to be.

Larissa stood in the kitchen washing dishes when Derrick's cell phone rang on the counter. She grabbed it and handed it to him where he sat on a nearby living room sofa. "Scooter?" she said sarcastically.

Derrick laughed. "It's a childhood nickname she had for me that somehow stuck," he explained as she returned to the sink.

Karen's voice sounded excited when Derrick answered. "Have you guys heard the news?" she asked.

"Not sure what you're talking about," Derrick answered.

"It's all over the national news, but check that Flagstaff website you told me about. Hurry!"

Now Derrick's heart thumped harder. The news had to be about Larissa, himself, or both of them for Karen to sound so urgent, but her voice hadn't been filled with dread; she actually sounded excited. How could that be? He reached for his nearby iPad and called Larissa to join him. By the time she settled on the sofa beside him, Derrick had the website loaded.

BREAKING NEWS flashed in red letters across the top of the screen. Underneath scrolled a headline: *Shocking Outburst in County Courthouse.*

"Oh my," Larissa exclaimed. "What on earth could this be?"

The video report began after Derrick tapped the screen. A middle-aged male reporter stood outside near the Coconino County Superior Court building on a blustery day. A few scattered snowflakes collected on his shoulders and others drifted to the ground around him. Behind the reporter, a few disinterested people conducting business of their own entered and exited the building along a walkway recently cleared of snow. As the wind blew his hair, the reporter spoke into a handheld microphone.

"A startling outburst occurred today in Coconino County Superior Court after accused murderer Warren Pickett entered a not guilty plea in the fatal stabbing of Amberwood businessman Albert Simmons. Pickett appeared agitated and uncooperative throughout the proceedings, then, when led away in shackles, he focused his attention on surrounding cameras."

The video image cut to the crowded courtroom. Tall and thin with shoulder-length stringy light brown hair and black-framed glasses, Pickett stared into the nearest camera and began his rant.

"I ain't done nothing wrong." He sneered into the camera, then flashed a wicked grin, exposing a mouthful of teeth in varying stages of decay. "You guys ain't as smart as you think you are. You got it wrong with that Baxter lady, and you got it wrong with me, too."

An off-screen voice asked, "What are you saying?"

Pickett laughed and said, "I know who really killed that Baxter jerk." He held up his shackled hands, formed a finger pistol with his right hand, pointed it directly at the camera, and shouted, "Bam! Bam! Two to the head!"

The video image cut back to the reporter outside of the building. "Authorities gave no comment on the disturbing statement, yet inside sources claim that certain officials expressed concern that there could be merit to Pickett's claim."

Now Larissa's mug shot filled the screen.

"A national manhunt continues for Larissa Baxter, who, shortly after being released on bail for the murder of her husband, Kenneth Baxter, apparently fled prosecution."

Derrick slumped back against the sofa. The news was astounding and could change everything. He tried to read Larissa's expression, but it registered nothing but shock. "One of us needs to say something," he finally broke the silence.

Larissa stiffened her stance, then relaxed. "I'm not getting my hopes up," she said. "This guy Pickett could be a total quack. I've never heard of him."

"I'm not so sure," Derrick said. "That remark about certain officials being concerned; a lot could be read into that."

"How's that?"

"Well, there's no way to be sure, but something that he said must reveal facts that only the killer or an accomplice would know." Derrick paused to ponder the development further. "They've focused entirely on you and apparently never considered the fact that maybe two other killers were involved."

Larissa took a deep breath. "It could possibly be good news," she said. "Since I didn't do it, I know for certain that someone else did. Maybe there was more than one killer."

Derrick's mind filled with sudden thoughts. Could Larissa be completely exonerated? If so, what would that mean? Would she take off like a bird from a cage without a second thought, leaving him to die a slow, agonizing death? For the first time since he'd met Larissa, he felt conflicted. Yes, he wanted what was best for her, but as his illness progressed, he felt himself growing more dependent on her. In fact, at this point he needed her as much as she needed him. How ironic it was that when he whisked her away, she was in dire need, and now the roles were reversing.

Of course, the wheels of justice turned slowly. Even if Pickett's comments had merit, time could drag on before it ever came to Larissa being absolved, and time was something he now had little of. He doubted that she would be free in his lifetime.

"Derrick—"

She broke his concentration.

"You were just staring into space and not saying anything."

He blushed. "I'm sorry," he said. "I was just overcome by the possibilities." A slight chill in the air reminded him it would soon be time for more firewood, and Derrick hoped he wouldn't feel exhausted after such a simple task.

Larissa exhaled deeply but still had a look of deep concern. "I guess we need to check the news every day from now on," she said.

CHAPTER TWENTY-EIGHT

arissa sensed Derrick's mood was noticeably different following the Flagstaff outburst. He seemed troubled, and that concerned her.

The possibility of being cleared of all charges was intriguing. It meant freedom—not from Derrick, but in terms of getting out and living again, no more feeling like a hamster running inside a wheel. What would she do if she were completely cleared? She knew that she wouldn't immediately take off and leave Derrick in the dust. After all, where would she go? She had grown accustomed to his company, and more and more she recognized that he was a decent man. She never felt threatened by him; in fact, she actually felt protected by him, and that was what made his lackluster reaction to the newscast most puzzling to her.

Larissa almost wished that the outburst hadn't occurred at all, that they could simply go back to the way things were before, at least for a while, but deep inside she knew that she had a whole life ahead of her. Besides, nothing would happen anytime soon, so she decided to just let it pass for now.

Over the next several days Larissa perceived Derrick becoming even more quiet and withdrawn. She knew he hadn't been feeling well and tried to leave him to himself, but curiosity about his divorce was getting to her, so she reached for a framed photo of a young bride and groom on the mantel above the fireplace and turned to him as he sat in his recliner staring blankly out the window across the water.

"I guess life was more innocent for all of us back when we were younger," she said.

"Huh?"

She held out the photo toward him. "Every bride and groom, · even if their marriage eventually ends up in divorce, look full of love and happiness on their wedding day. There's not even a clue of bad times ahead." She paused for a moment. "Although I would say without a doubt that my wedding day was far from the happiest moment of my life."

"Yeah," was all he said. Perhaps he was feeling worse than she thought, but she decided to push on.

"It's obvious how much you still love her, even after your divorce."

Derrick continued to stare vacantly ahead.

"I asked Karen what went wrong in your marriage, and she said that it needed to come from you."

Derrick groaned and said, "It's complicated."

Larissa sat on the cream-colored sofa, her favorite, and placed the framed photo beside her. "Everything's complicated," she said. She stared at him with an endearing expression, then said, "You know, we're sort of stuck here together for the time being. Wouldn't it be best if we opened up to each other a bit more?"

Derrick exhaled deeply and looked down, avoiding eye contact. "Would it really be that helpful?" he asked.

"Well, you know virtually everything about me. I think it's only fair that I know more about you."

When he glanced at her, she saw a growing sadness in his eyes. Perhaps she shouldn't be opening old wounds, but then he began to talk. "Only Karen knows the whole story. It's not easy to talk about."

"Please, Derrick."

He cleared his throat, and a lone tear trickled down his right cheek. "I must have been living in my own private, selfish world, not even knowing what was going on right under my nose," he began. "One day out of the clear blue sky, Sherry walked up to me and told me she wanted a divorce. I was sitting right there where you are, reading a magazine. At first I misunderstood and thought she meant someone we knew was getting a divorce, so I asked who.

"She laughed at me and said, '*Us*. We're getting a divorce.' I must have gone into shock because I don't remember much of what she said after that. It's mainly her tone of voice that comes to mind. It was cruel and heartless. I'd never heard her speak to me that way before. There was so much bitterness and resentment."

"You really didn't see it coming?" Larissa asked.

"Not in a million years," Derrick said. "I was totally clueless. I noticed that she had lost weight and was styling her hair differently. I thought she was prettying herself up for me. It never occurred to me that she had fallen in love with someone else."

"Oh, that's so sad, Derrick."

Now tears streamed from both eyes. "I've never experienced pain like that. It would have been better if she had stabbed me instead. Physical wounds are easier to heal." He stopped to clear his throat, and Larissa noticed for the first time that his voice had grown weaker. "She said she couldn't stand the sight of me anymore," he continued, "that she wanted more out of life than I could give her. I was devastated.

"She stormed away yelling more hurtful things at me, and I practically collapsed onto the sofa. I heard her car speed away, and I didn't know what to do. I started to call Karen to confide in her, but I couldn't even do that. I was such a mess that I sat here for hours feeling numb and helpless."

Larissa felt tears well in her own eyes. It was difficult watching Derrick relive such a painful moment. She regretted having broached the subject and wanted to go to him, to console him, but instead said, "Let's talk about something else."

Derrick slowly shook his head and said, "No, you need to hear the rest."

"There's more?"

Derrick swallowed hard and sniffled. "A few hours later, a dep-uty sheriff knocked on my door. He said . . . he told me . . . that Sherry had been involved in a terrible accident at Stemley Bridge. It must have happened right after she left here. He said that she was in intensive care at Baptist Medical Center in Talladega."

"Oh Derrick!"

"When I got there, she was in an induced coma. They were about to transfer her to the trauma unit at UAB Hospital in Birmingham. She had severe spinal injuries and would never walk again, if she lived at all."

Now Derrick was really weeping, heaving between his words. Larissa was, too. The memories were obviously hard for him to bear.

"What on earth did you do?"

"I stayed right by her side. Her friends and family came to visit her, and mine did, too. All the while I pretended that everything was normal between us, that her hateful words had never been spoken. When she regained consciousness, she was completely paralyzed. She would never walk or talk again."

"And you kept her horrible words a secret?"

"Of course I did!" Derrick snapped. "The empty bedroom on the middle level up there was where they set up her hospital bed and life support equipment. Her doc said she could live like that probably for a year or so, and I took good care of her. I really did."

"Oh, Derrick, how could you do that after she treated you so shamelessly?"

"Because I loved her. Sure, I was devastated, but love trumps all other feelings," he said, then paused briefly as if to gather his thoughts. "You know, love doesn't come with an on and off switch. It's easy to fall in love, and it can happen quickly, but falling out of love . . . well, that usually takes time. Sherry didn't just wake up one morning and realize that she didn't love me anymore. Her feelings for me changed over several months, if not years. But I was blindsided by it all. I couldn't just turn off my love for her, no matter what she said or did. I still loved her as much as I ever did, maybe even more."

"Wow!" Larissa said. "I never thought love could be so deep."

"Real love has no boundaries, as far as I'm concerned," he said.

Derrick wiped moisture from his cheeks onto his sleeve. "After just a few months she took a turn for the worse and passed away."

"How did you feel? I know it sounds awful, but wasn't there at least a slight sense of relief? I mean, caring for her twenty-four-seven must have been terribly hard on you."

He shook his head. "I wasn't ready to let her go," he said, "but there were definitely some stressful moments. I remember how she stared at me sometimes, and I wondered what was going through her mind or could she even think at all. Did she feel sorry for the horrible things she said to me? Did she appreciate how I was caring for her? Or was she just wishing that it was her lover standing over her instead of me?"

Larissa couldn't believe the feelings coming over her. She felt such deep compassion for Derrick that she wanted to hold him, to show him the warmth of embrace that he'd been missing for so long and so desperately deserved. Could she actually be developing feelings for him? Without a doubt things would never be the same between them after this.

"So whatever happened to this lover? Did you ever confront him?"

"I never knew who he was. He must have visited her in the hospital early on, but there were so many friends from her office and her social activities that it was just a blur. I was in such a state of shock that I wouldn't have noticed anyone showing more emotion than necessary. He must have been at her funeral, too. Whoever he was, he just vanished into the woodwork."

"Oh, that must have been maddening!"

"It was. I talked to a private detective once about finding out who he was. The detective was a good man. He told me that it shouldn't be too difficult to figure out but convinced me that it would only end up hurting me more in the long run. Some things just need to remain secrets. I agreed. After that I just tried to forget and move on. I was getting nowhere for several weeks, so I finally decided to go away for a while, back to Arizona. You know the rest."

In a moment of instant clarity, a revelation struck Larissa hard. No matter how strong someone's love, like Derrick's, might be, he could still be guilty of neglect, of not recognizing his wife's needs or making an effort to keep his marriage strong and healthy. She realized that she herself had been guilty of the same early on in her own marriage. She had focused entirely on Ken's faults, assigning all of the blame to him without stopping even for a moment to consider that she had made little to no effort to give Ken the support of a devoted wife. She'd never given her own marriage a chance.

It was a trap easy for anyone to fall into, even someone as seemingly perfect as Derrick. Perhaps Sherry had indeed had motivation to look elsewhere, but that didn't make it right. Had she been totally open with Derrick about what she felt was missing in their marriage, he would have at least had an opportunity to make amends. They could have worked on their relationship together. Larissa felt saddened by how easily an otherwise strong marriage deteriorated into emotional disaster.

Derrick stood, slowly walked to the sofa, and sat beside her, moving the photo to the coffee table. "Larissa," he said, "someday you'll find someone you truly love, someone who'll love you just as much. I learned something important that I want you to remember."

"Yes?" she said between sniffles.

"The secret of a happy marriage," he began, "is to never do or not do anything that will cause your partner to look elsewhere. Love has to be constantly nurtured. If it's neglected, it'll die like a beautiful flower wilting in the sun. Had I been more attentive, if I had been more involved in her life and her needs, none of it would have happened. Just remember that, will you?"

Larissa silently agreed and threw her arms around Derrick, hugging him long and hard. As they cried together and she patted him on the back, an unusual warmth spread through her body. She squeezed him tighter. How could she have ever committed to someone like Ken when there were men like Derrick in the world? There had been no one like him in her life before. Those kind of men were rare. No matter how negligent Derrick may have been in his marriage, Sherry still hadn't known what a prize she had in him. Larissa would never criticize Sherry to Derrick's face, but if she had tried harder to save the marriage, too, the result could have been different.

Larissa felt a growing bond with Derrick that she had never anticipated. Those many weeks ago on a lonely night in Arizona, the heart of the Old West, a stranger had drifted into town in a Chevy Tahoe rather than a horse, and the two of them had ridden off together into the sunset.

CHAPTER TWENTY-NINE

The lead story for Flagstaff was headlined *Pickett Defense Attorney Holds Revealing Press Conference.* The video loaded on Derrick's iPad and began to play.

A tall, thin, bald, immaculately dressed African American man stood at a podium and spoke into a microphone. Yellow text at the bottom of the screen read *Robert Danvers, Defense Attorney for Warren Pickett.*

Danvers began, "I've prepared a brief statement for my client, Warren Pickett. There will be no questions. Let me state from the beginning that I in no way endorse the following statement. I advised my client against making this information public, but to abide by his wishes I reluctantly do so.

"My client is charged with capital murder for the death of Albert Simmons. Mr. Pickett is innocent of all charges and is in good faith cooperating in the investigation of another crime for which he has not been promised any kind of deal or leniency. Mr. Pickett was originally included in a murder-for-hire plot arranged by Mr. Kenneth Baxter. The intended target was Mr. Baxter's wife, Larissa Baxter.

"Mr. Pickett states that two hired killers were included in the action because Mr. Baxter insisted, quote, 'I want to be sure the job gets done. I need two of you in case one of you effs something up,' unquote. Mr. Pickett held an extreme dislike for Mr. Baxter and backed out of the arrangement at the last minute. Mr. Pickett is a concerned citizen and will continue to assist this ongoing investigation. Thank you."

An attractive blonde anchorwoman at a studio anchor desk added, "A spokesperson for the Baxter family has issued a statement saying, 'These allegations have absolutely no merit and are an obvious attempt to embarrass the very criminal justice system that put Mr. Pickett behind bars in the first place. Prosecutors did, indeed, get it right in both instances.'

"Prosecutors in the Baxter case have made no comment as to whether or not these allegations warrant further investigation."

Larissa was stunned and momentarily speechless. Her heart sank.

"Wow," Derrick said. "Did you have any idea something like that was going on?"

Larissa slowly shook her head and covered her face with her hands. Stunned beyond belief, never in her wildest dreams had she imagined Ken being that evil. Yes, he was an awful man; she had suspected him of cheating on multiple occasions, and their marriage had felt like a sham practically from the beginning, but murder? A cold chill ran through her body; she had actually been the intended target! The more she thought about it, though, the more it made sense. Divorce would have been far too scandalous and shameful for the Baxter family, whereas Ken, as a widower, could have basked in the community's sympathy.

Feeling nauseous, Larissa began to shake. How close had she come to actually being killed? When would it have occurred, and how did Ken end up dead instead of her? Conflicting emotions overwhelmed her. In one instance she felt closer now to being vindicated, while at the same time she seemed more vulnerable than before. How could Ken have ever conceived of such a plan?

Tears welled in her eyes; she began to sob.

"Larissa?" Derrick interrupted her thoughts. "You're trembling. What can I do to help?"

She covered her face with her hands. "I'm okay," she said as she stood. "I just need some time alone."

Derrick felt helpless as Larissa slowly made her way upstairs to her room. He could only imagine how she must feel. Obviously,

Ken got exactly what he deserved, but how could it have possibly ended up the way it did? Had the hand of God caused Ken to be murdered before he could put his plan against Larissa into motion? Ken had been dealing with some despicable people. If you sleep with the devil, you'll eventually get burned, someone once said.

As moonlit shadows from trees twisted and bent across the living room floor and furniture, Derrick heard Larissa still crying upstairs, but felt that he shouldn't disturb her. What was in store for her now? Pickett's statement to the press could send the investigation in an entirely different direction, and it now seemed more possible than ever that Larissa could be vindicated. Would it happen in his lifetime?

Derrick's heart ached. He couldn't stand the sound of her misery, especially when there was nothing he could do to comfort her. Tears accumulated in his own eyes as he realized more and more the depth to which his feelings for her had grown. With a weak smile, he thought of the irony of how love could come quickly or it could slowly sneak up on you when you least expected it. Sometimes love could lurk in your heart, waiting to make itself known.

Suddenly Derrick felt a peaceful glow throughout his body, overcoming him like a divine presence. He had never questioned why God had decided to take him at this time, but without a doubt God had given him the greatest feeling of all, a growing love different from any he'd previously known, to enhance his life as his body slowly approached the finish line.

He couldn't imagine a better way to leave this earth.

CHAPTER THIRTY

Fishing boats rarely stirred up enough wake to rock the floating pier, especially this time of year, but it gently bobbed up and down today. It was another unusually warm mid-December day as Larissa sat on the edge of the pier. Derrick lay on his back on a towel beside her, a cushion beneath his head.

Enough hair had grown back on Larissa's scalp for the morning wind to ruffle it. Dark rain clouds appeared across the lake, a stiff breeze building. Derrick gazed across the water at the storm brewing and said, "We can't stay here long. Heavy rain is headed this way."

Ignoring Derrick's warning, Larissa gazed at her surroundings and said, "This really is a beautiful place."

"I've been blessed, there's no doubt about it," Derrick said.

Larissa turned around to look at him. "I've only seen you pray once, at Thanksgiving. Are you really such a strong believer?" she asked.

"Of course I am!" Derrick answered. "I pray every day, usually more than once. In fact, it's often several times a day. I just pray silently."

In the distance a train whistle wailed a lonely tune; a low rumble of thunder sounded across the water and shook the dock. Derrick sat up beside her. "You've never been a believer?" he asked.

"No, not really."

Derrick scooted a bit closer until their elbows touched. "So you think it's just a coincidence that you and I are here together?"

She paused for a moment, then said, "Yes, I guess I do."

Derrick dipped his feet into the cold water, looked down, then gazed across the rising waves at the approaching storm. "I don't believe in coincidences."

"Why not?"

"Well, if it's hard for you to believe in a higher power, it's just as difficult for me to believe in coincidences."

Larissa slowly shook her head. "Derrick, sometimes things just happen. There doesn't have to be a reason."

"Okay then, look at it this way. Was it a coincidence that once upon a time I briefly lived in Arizona? And that I just happened to meet your father there? That he just happened to say something to me about your family situation, and I just happened to remember it years later when I just happened to be back in Arizona briefly and just happened to see your story in the news? And by the way, I wasn't searching for Arizona news at the time. I was looking for news from back home, but my browser knew my location and gave me the local Flagstaff news instead.

"And even more than all of that, one coincidence piled on top of another, how did I come up with such a crazy rescue plan that's so uncharacteristic of me, something that I could never have conceived of doing, that brought the two of us together? Where did such a preposterous idea come from? It just popped into my head, as if it wasn't even my own thought." Derrick stopped for a brief laugh. "I don't know, Larissa. It's harder for me to believe that so many coincidences just happened to align together at the precise moments to bring us to this point than it is to believe that a Supreme Being made it all happen."

"Hmm," Larissa said, "that's a good point, but—"

A long bolt of lightning sizzled across the sky, followed by an explosive boom of thunder and the smell of ozone. A stiff wind whisked across the water and rattled the pine needles of nearby trees. Falling pine cones pelted the ground. Derrick took a deep breath and nudged Larissa with his elbow, pointing across the water in the distance. "Watch this," he said. "I've only seen it happen once before."

Rain fell heavily on the distant side of the lake, almost a mile away, and slowly edged toward them in the fading light. "When it gets halfway across the lake we'll need to make a run for it."

Larissa leaned against him, seemingly mesmerized by the approaching rainfall. It was like a curtain of water slowly sweeping toward them. Derrick stood, reached down for her hand, and struggled to help her up. "We'd better run," he said, trying to catch his breath.

Before they reached land at the end of the pier, the simultaneous sounds of Dixie racing up the driveway barking and a car speeding much too fast along the narrow roadway connecting to his private entrance sounded worrisome. A loud thump echoed down the driveway, then a screeching yelp, and the blood drained from Derrick's face. "DIXIE!" he yelled.

The car sped away, but the yelping grew louder, more intense, then gradually changed to an agonizing wail. Larissa helped Derrick along, and they ran toward the injured dog as the rain caught up with them. Larissa had to slow down for Derrick; he couldn't move nearly as quickly as he once did, and their feet lost traction on the wet driveway. "No!" he said as he huffed. "Please, God, no!"

By the time they reached Dixie, she lay motionless on her side, blood spreading around her head beside the now rain-slicked road, her eyes barely open. Derrick leaned over her in the knee-high brush, gently rubbing her furry head as tears streamed down his face and a heavy rain pounded him on the back. Larissa looked on in horror, her face red and puffy with as many tears as Derrick. Their clothing was already drenched, but that was the least of their concerns.

"Dixie girl," Derrick said soothingly, "hang on while I get the car." He stood and slowly began to make his way back down the driveway.

"Derrick, wait!" Larissa called to him over the driving rain. "It's too late to take her to the vet. You need to spend her final moments with her."

Dixie's breathing slowed with a trickle of blood oozing from her mouth as Derrick returned to lie beside her in the soaked weeds. Her blank stare froze, her eyes glazed, rolled up into her head, and she grew perfectly still.

"Oh Derrick," Larissa said as she gently patted Dixie's side.

"It's okay, girl," Derrick mumbled to Dixie. "It's your time to go. It's okay."

Dixie grunted and took her final breath. Derrick collapsed on top of her, oblivious to the cold rain still drenching him, then Larissa lay against him. There were no words to be said. Derrick had suffered yet another loss.

The ride home from having Dixie cremated was long and silent. Both Derrick and Larissa were still overwhelmed with grief when Larissa finally said, "Don't you think it's ironic that this happened while we were talking about—"

"Don't say it," Derrick interrupted. "I know what you're thinking." He gripped the steering wheel harder and stared straight ahead. "God doesn't make bad things happen. People do."

Larissa paused briefly and pinched the bridge of her nose. "But aren't you just the slightest bit angry with God?"

Derrick glanced at her, then returned his attention to the road ahead. "Like I said, it's not God's fault. *People* make bad things happen, like that idiot who was driving too fast. God didn't make him drive that way, and God didn't make Dixie get in his way. It was free will in both instances." He swallowed hard, then continued, "It's moments like this when people need God the most. Or at least I do."

Following a moment of silence, Derrick's expression turned ominously more despondent. Larissa obviously noticed and asked, "What's wrong?"

He exhaled and shook his head, hating to admit that he'd made a mistake, but she deserved to know, no matter how difficult it was to speak. "I . . . should have brought her ashes back. She deserved a final resting place here at the lake."

Slowly nodding, Larissa placed her left hand on Derrick's right knee. "Don't second-guess yourself. This was a traumatic experience, and you did the best that you could under the circumstances."

Derrick now nodded as well, his face showing a sense of relief. Larissa patted his knee. "You're a good man, Derrick Walton. Bad things shouldn't happen to you."

"You're a good woman, too, Larissa. You've just made some bad choices. We all have."

She nodded but said nothing.

"I've seen so much unrest in my lifetime. Both in my personal life and throughout the whole world," Derrick said. "I just wish people would stop judging each other and try to live together in peace."

"I know what you mean. But in my case I deserve some judgment, most of it anyway."

Derrick exhaled deeply and massaged his forehead, then said, "I won't preach to you anymore, Larissa. It's your life and your decision. I just hope someday you'll at least have a more open mind about your Creator."

She had a vacant look in her eyes, and Derrick had no idea if he had gotten through to her at all.

An eerie silence hung over the house all afternoon and into the night. Although Dixie had been an outdoor dog, she was frequently heard barking at one thing or another in the yard. Her focus had always been on the door, and she had never missed an opportunity to welcome Derrick or Larissa when either stepped outside.

Larissa remembered watching Derrick brush his fingertips down Dixie's back, scrubbing her thick black fur, patting her big head and hugging her tightly. He obviously loved that dog, and Dixie had loved him. She surmised from Derrick's actions that he undoubtedly had been an affectionate, loving husband. He definitely demonstrated a strong allegiance toward anyone, or anything, he loved. Again, Sherry hadn't realized how lucky she had been to have him, regardless of any shortcomings.

Now Larissa lay in bed staring into the dark of night, listening to rustling limbs in a nearby pine sway in the wind and brush against the side of the house. The rain had stopped and a cold front had swept in, a harder blast of wind thumping against an exterior wall. For the first time in her life, Larissa truly felt isolated. Had something been triggered by the loss of Dixie? She had no idea, only that she detested this empty feeling.

As her mind continued to race, she realized how much Dixie had meant to her, too. She had never been an animal person, had never owned a pet as a child nor as an adult, but there was something about Dixie that had gradually tugged at her heart. If she felt this strongly about the loss of that mangy dog, she could only imagine how Derrick must be hurting.

Before giving it any further thought, she called out to him downstairs, "Derrick, are you awake?" She knew that he was. The house was small enough that he would have no problem hearing her.

"Yes," he finally answered.

Larissa hesitated, contemplating what she was about to say, then decided to go with her heart. "We don't need to be alone tonight," she said. "Will you come up and stay with me, just this once?"

He didn't answer right away. Had he heard her? "Derrick?" she called out to him.

"Are you sure?" he answered.

"Yes, Derrick. I feel awful. Just this once, okay?"

He didn't answer, but moments later she heard him slowly trudging up the stairs. He silently slid into bed beside her wearing the same worn flannel shirt with holes in the sleeves that she had seen before. He lay perfectly still, and she could tell he was nervous.

"It's okay, Derrick," she said. "It's been a traumatic day."

Derrick exhaled, then said, "It's way too quiet around here. I can't stand it."

"I know," she said, "but let's just try to get some sleep."

They lay there silently, each deep in their own thoughts, until finally sleep overtook them.

CHAPTER THIRTY-ONE

"**J**ust this once" became forever.

Derrick was puzzled as he lay beside Larissa several nights later. He couldn't imagine that she had any physical interest in him, but he had begun to suspect that she did have feelings of some kind. He was enormously attracted to her, and even though he loved her, he accepted that boundaries must be observed. There was no room for love under the fragile conditions they lived in. Even if she also loved him, there was no way it could fully develop.

He took a deep breath and exhaled. Aside from love, he was only human, and despite his diminished libido, he felt a bonding warmth as he listened to her breathing and when she occasionally rolled over in her sleep and brushed against him.

His health had deteriorated rapidly following the loss of Dixie, and he wondered if Larissa had even noticed. Derrick imagined what it could have been like to have been in a relationship with someone as beautiful as she. He knew that he was only average looking at best, yet Sherry had married him, and she had always been pretty. When they attended functions together, Derrick had always taken pride in the fact that his wife stood out among the rest. He realized once again how much he had taken Sherry for granted.

His attraction to Larissa had changed since they first met. Now he saw her as a complete individual rather than just a beautiful but spoiled woman in jeopardy. She might have been gorgeous, but she hadn't been without difficulties in life. Her looks had been about the only thing going for her, and now she had been forced to discount even that.

He wondered if he would be handling these circumstances differently if he still had more life ahead. He hadn't considered telling her about his health issues before now; he hadn't expected the two of them to be together this long. He still wondered to what degree his future would even matter to her.

He lay awake this particular night long after she had gone to sleep. The pain of losing Dixie had subsided somewhat, and he had tried to focus on the situation at hand. He thought about the latest developments in Flagstaff and wondered once again what Larissa might do if the charges were eventually dropped. Of course she would return to Flagstaff . . . or would she?

Larissa had opened up to him completely, or so he thought, and she had never given even the slightest hint that she missed anything about her former life. Maybe her previous experiences had been so negative that she might want to stay away from Arizona to avoid bad memories, but where would she go instead? Vegas was the only option that came to mind, yet her life there hadn't been altogether pleasant either. He prayed she would leave that part of her past behind.

None of it mattered anyway. He could feel his body changing, slowly withering away. In one respect he was tempted to see a doctor to learn approximately how much time he had left. On the other hand, however, he felt it might be best not to know. Larissa's charges may not even be dropped in his lifetime, if ever, and there would certainly be no future for him with her regardless of what either of them wanted.

Derrick got little sleep that night but felt a sense of peace. Seeing the breaking news from Flagstaff reinforced his decision to rescue Larissa, that he had done the right thing. If he hadn't, her husband's killer could have returned to finish the job. He shuddered at the thought. He had put his life at risk to help someone he didn't even know, without even the slightest hint that he might eventually fall in love with her, and regardless of the eventual outcome, Derrick felt good about himself for sacrificing his own freedom to help someone in trouble. By saving her, he had saved himself as well. God indeed had a plan for him yet.

CHAPTER THIRTY-TWO

After another long day of virtual confinement, the two sat in the living room watching the sun set, Larissa this time in the recliner at the window and Derrick partially covered by a blanket, on the dark and worn sofa. Ending his call with Karen, he glanced at Larissa with a look of sadness. "She obviously doesn't understand how much Dixie meant to me," he said.

Twisting the recliner toward him, Larissa was confused. "What do you mean?" she asked.

Derrick took a deep breath and explained, "Oh sure, she expressed her condolences alright, but she was quick to shift the conversation back to me. She didn't seem to pick up at all how upset I am over losing Dixie."

Pondering her best response, Larissa took a moment before answering. "In her defense, though, she hasn't seen you loving Dixie like I have. To her, Dixie might have just seemed like a mutt that you rescued. She couldn't have understood the bond you had with that dog, especially not being a dog-lover herself."

Wiping a tear from his eye, Derrick concurred. "I guess you're right. Thanks."

As the sunset lingered, the temperature was a bit too cool to sit outside on the deck. Brilliant colors of purple, orange, and red blazed across the sky, reflecting across the lake, the view stunning.

After dinner and a long movie, they sat on the sofa together, huddled beneath a blanket. Larissa had something to say.

She hadn't noticed how much weight Derrick had lost until he began to sleep with her. His body almost seemed frail, and she was ready to confront him about it, but at the last minute decided this wasn't the right time. It was getting late, and a serious conversation at this hour would likely keep them both awake. Instead, she decided to bring up something else that she'd been thinking about.

"Remember our talk on the pier," she asked, "about everything happening for a reason?"

"Yes?" he answered sleepily.

Larissa turned to face Derrick, clearly not as sleepy as he was. "Do you honestly believe that millions, if not billions, of people pray to God at the same time, and that He listens and responds to each one individually? No matter what you say, Derrick, that stretches the imagination."

Derrick seemed more awake and perky now, obviously happy that she had brought up this discussion. "That's a great question," he answered. "Let me show you something."

He reached for his smartphone on the arm of the sofa. "Oh, do you have God's personal phone number or do you guys only Tweet?" she said jokingly.

"Just listen," he said.

Derrick opened Google Maps and punched in Flagstaff, Arizona. Up popped a suggested route with a couple of alternates, ready for him to press the navigation button for voice directions. "Millions of people use GPS at the same time," he said. "I don't understand the technology, but somehow a satellite or something receives each request individually and gives made-to-order feedback to help users get where they're going. Again, millions of people, at the same, getting personalized answers."

Larissa stared at him in the dim light, listening intently.

"God gave man the brains to figure out how to do that," he continued. "Now, if He allowed man to accomplish something this significant, it doesn't take a stretch of the imagination to know that He himself can do astronomically greater things on

His own, so listening to millions or billions of prayers and answering them individually seems like a snap for the Creator of the universe."

"You're actually making sense . . . again," she said, "except that he doesn't always answer prayers."

"Ah, but He does," Derrick interjected. "He may not answer them the way you want Him to or when you want Him to, but He always listens and looks out for all of us, even unbelievers."

With a chill in the air, Larissa pulled the blanket tighter under her chin. "Sounds like a convenient answer to me."

Derrick cleared his throat, apparently enjoying the conversation. "I know you're not a Garth Brooks fan, so I suppose you've never heard his song 'Unanswered Prayers.' "

"No, country music is pretty far down my list," she said.

Derrick laughed. "That's another of your Southern prejudices sneaking through, thinking that all country music is about drinking beer, driving trucks, and chasing women. Garth's song explains that God knows what's best for us. Sometimes what you want isn't at all what you need. You'll realize later in life that God was right when he didn't answer a particular prayer."

"Garth says this, huh?"

"Garth's a smart man. A lot of other country artists are, too. I think they're more tuned in to the life of the average hardworking American than other singers—but that's just my opinion. I hope you're learning similar life lessons from your hip-hop."

Larissa yawned. "Okay," she said as she pulled away from him and stood to go upstairs. "I'm tired of these discussions. You always seem to have an answer that's hard to come back at."

Derrick smiled and patted her on the bottom.

"Jesus loves you," he said.

Thoughts of his own mortality finally struck Derrick like a dagger in the heart. Throughout his life he'd had a tendency to focus on memories of the bad times he'd experienced; now he realized how many good times there had been and almost regretted his decision to refuse treatment. As he gazed out the window at sparkles of moonlight reflecting on the water, it dawned on him to an even greater extent how truly precious life was. His doctors couldn't have saved him, but they could likely have given him more time, and that was now something he was rapidly running out of.

Losing Dixie had been a crushing blow. Her death, however, had been a catalyst for his growing relationship with Larissa, but now there was an increasing possibility that she would be set free, so he could conceivably lose her as well. He hoped he would pass away before that happened. Still, if treatment had been able to give him one more day with her, it would have been worth it.

He felt like a hypocrite having had talks of God with Larissa when he himself hadn't asked God for healing as his health deteriorated. He wanted to be strong now and live out the remainder of his life to the fullest, but in his constantly weakening state that could be quite the challenge. Besides, he somehow knew with all certainly that it was time for him to be called to heaven, so it seemed pointless to ask God to change His mind.

CHAPTER THIRTY-THREE

A s Larissa was once again working out in the living room, she heard the jingle of Derrick's keys before seeing him walk toward the door. Almost out of breath from the exertion, she gazed up to him and asked, "Where are you going?"

He stopped and stared down over the cedar railing at her. "To pick up a few groceries," he answered.

Feeling overwhelmed by claustrophobia, she called out, "Wait a minute. I'll go with you."

Derrick rolled his eyes. "You know that still may not be a good idea," he complained in a weak voice as she made her way up to face him, towel in hand.

Her skin and hair damp with sweat, she took a deep breath, then complained, "Well, it's not a good idea for me to stay locked inside this long either. I feel like I'm in prison after all."

Derrick looked irritated. Shaking his head, he said, "Do you really think it's worth the risk just for a short trip to Publix?"

Anger boiled inside her as she countered, "Maybe I do. I can slump down in the seat while you're inside. No one will see me." She hesitated, trying to gauge his expression, then added, "Just wait while I change clothes."

As she turned to go upstairs, Derrick yelled in a stern voice, "Larissa! I won't let you jeopardize yourself. Maybe you can go out with me later, but not today."

Pivoting in her tracks, her face red with fury, she screamed, "Oh, so now you've decided to tell me what to do?"

"Larissa, I—"

"Just forget it," she screamed. "Maybe I'll still be here when you get back." She then stomped upstairs, swinging her towel wildly in the air and slamming the door.

Inside her bedroom at the adjoining bath, she snatched the shower curtain aside to turn the water on and heard him downstairs calling to her, "Larissa, it's up to you. If it's that important--"

"Just forget it!" she screamed again, fuming as she shut the water back off. *I've got to get out of here.*

No sooner had the sound of Derrick's Tahoe faded into the distance than Larissa furiously stomped outside the house. Enraged, her temper still out of control and feeling defiant, she headed toward the steep driveway, oblivious to wearing only her workout attire that covered little and offered almost no protection from the elements. The only occasion when she'd been up the driveway previously had been when Dixie was struck by a car. The steep ascent challenged her lungs, but her anger was so intense that she hardly noticed that or the cold.

At the top of the driveway she decided to turn left. Derrick would return from the right, and she didn't want him to happen upon her, preferring instead that if she stayed away long enough, he would arrive at a vacant house. It would serve him right. As she walked along the narrow road farther away, she noticed that several homes on the water to her left were much more affluent, bigger, and nicer than Derrick's, but their view of the lake was nothing comparable to his. Not a sign of life was visible at any of the houses, attesting to the seasonal appeal of the lakeside community.

When her anger subsided, she felt the chill of a cold wind freezing her breath, producing goose bumps on her arms and legs. Larissa began to shiver, and as she grew more uncomfortable, she calmed down and realized how silly she had been to storm away from the house in the cold. She was hurting no one but herself.

Cursing silently, she pivoted to return home only to spot two large dogs charging through the woods toward her, growling viciously. She knew little to nothing about dogs, but these were big. One had pointed ears, drooping jowls, and long legs. The other looked like a police dog, only scruffy. Paralyzed with fear, she tried to figure out a way to protect herself. Both canines appeared undernourished and in poor health, obviously strays intent on attacking her. If Dixie were still alive, she would be protected, but now—

Teeth gnashing, the dogs were almost upon her when she noticed a deep drainage ditch at the side of the road. She had to move quickly. In sheer panic, she braced herself to slide down the embankment about six feet to the bottom. Saliva from one of the dogs splattered against her neck as she started her narrow descent. Its teeth snapping so close to her shoulders made her thankful that she hadn't worn one of Derrick's jackets after all; otherwise, the dog likely could have grabbed the collar and possibly yanked her back up out of the ditch to rip her apart.

As Larissa dropped to the bottom, her arms and legs scraped against rocks jutting out from the ground. Hopefully, neither of the dogs would follow her down. The bottom of the ditch held about an inch or two of standing water and mud, but at least she felt safe for the moment, out of reach of the menacing beasts that remained at the top of the trough glaring down at her with vengeance.

The charging animals refused to give up, snarling ferociously from above, saliva dripping from their mouths. Could they possibly be rabid? Now she began to shiver, both from the cold and from fear. Her tight polyester shorts were ripped on the backside from the slide down; tiny trickles of blood ran from her arms and legs. Her wounds weren't serious, but she worried about hypothermia if she wasn't rescued soon.

How could I have been so stupid? she silently scolded herself. *How long has Derrick been gone?* Would he find her before she needed medical attention? Her tantrum could cause her to blow her cover and put both herself and Derrick in peril of being exposed if she needed to see a doctor.

Unexpectedly, the dogs' attention became diverted elsewhere, and they charged farther down the road, away from the ditch, their relentless barking fading in the distance. Larissa trembled as she tried to get a foothold on the side of the trench to climb out, but her muddy shoes prevented her from gaining any traction. This time the front of her body slid against the rocky side of the ditch. Feeling the pressure of the rocks scraping her knees, she winced as a particularly large stone jammed against her right breast, ripping her nylon sports bra and causing a surge of pain. This simply wasn't working.

Her panic intensifying, Larissa felt her heart thumping and her arms and legs, especially her feet, growing numb from the cold. Stumbling backward at the bottom of the ditch, she fell against the opposite side of the trench and slipped down, her bottom splashing into the muddy puddle below.

As she grew colder and more frightened, Larissa berated herself for having been so careless and allowing her temper to get the best of her.

Driving home, Derrick felt his energy quickly draining. Something was wrong. Previously, his condition had worsened slowly, almost undetectable, but now, without warning, it had accelerated, and he was anxious to get back to the comfort and security of his home. Hopefully Larissa had cooled off by now.

Bringing the Tahoe to a stop in the driveway, Derrick took a moment to catch his breath. Deep inhalations helped somewhat, but he wasn't sure if he had the strength to unload all of the groceries. He grabbed a couple of the lighter bags and slowly trudged to the door, hyperventilating along the way.

Once inside, he called out, "Larissa? I'm back." No response. "Larissa?" When his second summons produced no reaction, Derrick immediately grew concerned. She had been more angry than he'd ever seen her when he'd left; could she have held true to her threat and left the house? There was nowhere for her to go. The thought was chilling.

Depositing the groceries onto the small dining table, he looked around, called to her again, and saw no sign of her presence. She had left. He should have known better than to leave her so irate.

She couldn't have gone far on foot and wouldn't likely have been seen by anyone unless someone searching for lakefront property happened by. Any other time it would have been a simple task to drive around the primary road to find her, but feeling as weak as he did, Derrick wasn't sure what he was physically capable of. Also, it was getting colder outside, and a few raindrops had splattered against the windshield a couple of miles back. If the rain was headed this direction, it wouldn't bode well for Larissa, though it should force her to return home.

Hopefully she'd had the presence of mind to grab one of his heavy coats before leaving. He could check in his upstairs closet to see if one was missing, but that would only take away more precious time and drain more of his energy climbing the stairs; energy that could be put to better use searching for her instead. He swallowed hard, then started his slow trek back to the Tahoe.

Cold raindrops pelted against her exposed skin. Larissa shivered, cursing herself again for not dressing warmer. The abrasions on her arms and legs that had been painful only moments ago now felt numb from the cold. She knew that she couldn't stand this much longer.

In all the time she had been in this tomb-like pit she hadn't heard a single sign of life anywhere around her, only crows cawing from the treetops, a testament to how isolated the area was in winter—a stark contrast to how lively the place must be in mid-summer.

Freezing and exasperated, she rested her back against the far side of the ditch and waited.

Time passed slowly and miserably. Her teeth chattered. Should she try again to climb out? She scanned both sides of the ditch in search of an outcropping of larger rocks to grasp and pull herself out when she heard the distant whine of a vehicle heading her way.

What should she do? Most of her energy was depleted. The best she could do at this point was to hopefully jump high enough from the bottom to catch the driver's attention as the vehicle approached.

The car moved slowly, as if its driver were searching for something. Could it be Derrick?

Having guessed the direction Larissa had walked, Derrick slowly made his way farther away from the house, watching for any sign of her along the road or in the woods to the right. Feeling his nerves forcing him to a higher level of anxiety and his breath quickening, he finally spotted a pair of waving hands rapidly rising and falling, someone jumping from the depths of a drainage ditch to the right. It had to be her!

How could she have fallen into the pit? Regardless of how or why, he stopped the Tahoe and got out to confront her, ready to scold her for being so reckless.

Larissa had never been so happy to see anyone in her entire life when Derrick peered over the edge of the ditch, but his face bore a grimace. Of course he was angry with her, but now was not the time to be reprimanded. She desperately needed to get out of this situation.

"Derrick, please," she began between sobs. "You can be mad at me all you want when we get back to the house, but I'm freezing and I'm hurt, and I need to get out of here *now!*"

He stood motionless, and it was then that she realized he looked different from when he left. Something was wrong with him. His face had changed; his stature seemed weaker, his shoulders sagged. He wobbled unsteadily on his feet, examining the area, looking for something.

"I . . . I . . . don't think I'm strong enough . . . to pull you out. We'll have to find some other way." He glanced down the road toward his house, then said, "Follow me."

As Derrick slowly stumbled along the road, Larissa kept up with him below at the bottom of the ditch. A massive concrete culvert ahead ran under an unimproved entrance leading to an undeveloped lot. *Why didn't I think of walking back down the trench?* she admonished herself. At the mouth of the culvert she splashed through a wide pool of slush about six inches deep, coating her legs with mud. Barely able to grasp the top of the giant drainage pipe, she pulled herself up to the top, reached out for his assistance, then, leaning against him, Larissa gave him a major hug and mumbled into his chest, "I'm sorry, Derrick. This was so stupid of me."

Escorting her back to the Tahoe, Derrick wrapped his heavy jacket around her but remained speechless as he helped her into the passenger seat, not at all his usual self. "I was attacked by two huge dogs. I had to get into the ditch to escape."

Derrick harrumphed as he turned the Tahoe around and headed back toward home. Larissa saw that he was breathing hard. "And would this have happened if you had stayed at home like you should have?" he asked.

After wiping tears from her cheeks and shrugging further into Derrick's jacket, she apologized. "I'm sorry. I really am. I let my anger get away from me. It won't happen again."

CHAPTER THIRTY-FOUR

Derrick remained silent until the Tahoe came to a stop in the driveway. Without a doubt Larissa knew that his health had taken a sudden nosedive. He looked pale and weak. For the first time she realized that something could be seriously wrong with him.

While Derrick switched off the ignition and caught his breath, Larissa, her rage having long since subsided, was struck with a moment of sadness at the absence of Dixie's welcoming bark as the big Lab bounded excitedly toward the Tahoe to greet Derrick.

He slammed the driver's side door and stepped to the rear of the vehicle to retrieve groceries while Larissa stood outside the passenger door cleaning the seat, brushing away twigs and tiny pebbles that had fallen from her soiled, wet clothing. She would need to scrub the seat to remove the mud stains. Distracted by her cleaning efforts, when she looked up Derrick had managed to slip inside the house. Grabbing a couple more bags of groceries from the back and quickly catching up to him, Larissa met him in the hallway, remembering that her torn clothing exposed more of herself than Derrick had ever seen, but he hardly noticed.

"I'll get the rest," she said as she stepped past him. He wasn't carrying much, yet she noted the redness of his face and how slowly he moved. He appeared exhausted from such minor effort, and Larissa realized it was the first time he hadn't refused her help. When she'd initially arrived here, he had forbidden her from doing much of anything that he considered a "man's" job, but now it was different. Derrick continued inside without saying a word, apparently breathing so hard that he could barely speak.

Gathering the rest of the grocery bags from the Tahoe's cargo space, Larissa knew that, despite her own situation, she could no longer delay talking to Derrick about his failing health. She had noticed it for weeks now but had resisted commenting about it for fear it might embarrass him. She had learned that he was a proud man, and admitting weakness could be difficult for him.

A private telephone conversation with Karen earlier in the day while Derrick was otherwise distracted had yielded no answers about his condition. His sister sounded seriously concerned about her brother's health, but if she knew anything at all, she refused to violate his confidence. In fact, Karen responded with a request of her own; if Derrick revealed anything to Larissa about his health, would she please share the information with her, his only living relative? Unless Derrick specifically asked her not to, Larissa agreed to keep Karen informed.

Now, worried more than ever, she wanted him to know that he had her support. She wanted to be there for him as he had been for her. Hopefully he wouldn't be stubborn about seeking medical attention. After all, why wouldn't he want to feel better? Probably, with the proper medication or treatment, he could be good as new soon.

She deposited the final bags onto the kitchen table with the others. This house seemed more and more like home, and she had no interest in being anywhere else at the moment.

Derrick struggled to his feet, saying, "I'll help get the cold items into the refrigerator."

Larissa waved him away as she put gallon jugs of iced tea and milk away, then said, "The rest can wait. After I clean up we need to talk."

"Oh . . ." Derrick said, "more news from Flagstaff?"

"No . . . something else."

She hurried upstairs, all the while mulling over in her mind what she would say to him. Stripping off her destroyed shorts and top, she relished in the warmth of a hot shower. The cuts on her arms and legs didn't seem as bad as she had thought and would require no medical attention.

Pulling Derrick's long Crimson Tide shirt over her head and scrubbing her wet hair dry with a towel, she took a deep breath and headed back downstairs, dreading the upcoming confrontation.

Derrick lay slumped against the back of the sofa, his eyes closed, struggling to catch his breath. He glanced up at her as she entered the living room and asked, "So what's up?"

"You," she answered.

He made a puzzled expression, and Larissa put her hand on his knee. "I'm not so self-centered that I haven't noticed, Derrick," she said. "What's up with your health?"

"What do you mean?"

Larissa felt her anger rise. "Are you in denial or are you deliberately lying to me?" she said.

Derrick hung his head.

"Why haven't you seen a doctor?" she asked. "Don't you want to feel better?" She paused for his response, but it never came. "You came into my life to help me. Now you're not healthy enough to help anyone. Why are you so stubborn? It's not a big deal to see a doctor."

"It's not that I'm stubborn," Derrick snapped. "I know what's wrong with me, and seeing a doctor won't help."

Larissa rolled her eyes and said, "Of course a doctor can! You're smarter than that!"

She watched in confusion as tears welled in his eyes. He put his right hand over hers on his knee. "Larissa . . ." he began. "I should have told you before now, but the right opportunity never came up. I guess this is finally the time."

She felt a cold chill of dread wash through her body. Her heart sank. This wasn't going in the direction she'd hoped.

"There's no easier way to say it, but . . . I'm dying. I don't have a lot of time left."

Did she just hear that correctly? "Wait! What did you say?"

"It's true," he answered dejectedly, expelling a burst of pent-up air. "I may not have much time left."

Anger rose within Larissa as she jerked away from him. "Derrick, you've never lied to me before; at least, I don't think you have."

He appeared confused. "Why would you think that?"

Larissa exhaled, trying to keep her temper under control. "I'm not a moron," she said sarcastically. "I've known that you haven't been feeling well for a while now, but I haven't seen a single sign from you that your life was almost over. People don't act like it's business as usual when they're dying. They're depressed, and they have a bucket list. Why would you say such a thing to me, Derrick? Are you having a mental breakdown?"

Derrick reached out to her, but Larissa held her ground. He swallowed hard, then answered, "I would never lie to you, Larissa. You know me better than that."

She was seething, refusing to budge. "Then you owe me an explanation, mister," she demanded.

Derrick reached out for her hand, and she reluctantly took it. She felt herself begin to shake. Was her world crumbling around her? What if, just as she began to have strong feelings for this man, Derrick turned out to be delusional or deceitful after all they'd been through? It didn't seem fair.

Derrick cleared his throat, then weakly continued. "Believers don't fear death, Larissa. Death is just a transition point. It's just the next step toward eternal happiness."

Larissa was stunned to silence.

"It's just a way of life that believers follow."

"I don't buy it. You've got to help me understand."

Derrick appeared to be in deep thought, then explained, "When I was a kid, I went to Six Flags Over Georgia several times. Did you ever go to a big amusement park like that?"

Having no idea where he was going with this story, and hoping once again that his mental health hadn't suffered, she answered, "I went to Disneyland once when I was nine years old. It was one of the most exciting days of my life."

"Okay, good," Derrick continued. "Remember that massive parking lot that was so far from the park entrance that trams came to pick you up to give you a ride to the gate?"

"Yes?"

"It seemed like that tram ride would never end until we reached those magical thrill rides on the other side. Well, a believer's life is sort of like that tram ride. We try to make the best of that short journey, but our eyes are on the prize at the end, a life of eternal happiness in heaven—our spiritual amusement park."

Larissa slowly shook her head. "So you're telling me that the life of a believer is of no more significance than an amusement park tram ride?"

Derrick nodded and raised his eyebrows. "Life is great, and it must be treasured, but in the overall scheme of things, our life on earth is just a blip on the radar. I've had a good life, but I'm excited about what lies ahead, just like when I was a kid getting closer and closer to the park entrance," he said without skipping a beat.

"That's so hard to understand. How can there be no sadness in dying?" she asked.

"Oh sure, there's definitely some sadness," he continued. "I'll miss Karen . . . and I'll miss you, too. But I believe we'll all meet again when your time is up."

It was beginning to make more sense, the more she thought about it, although the news was still devastating. "I don't need a bucket list," Derrick added. "God has been good to me, and I've done everything that was important to me, but I'm a simple man. I've always been contented with what I have."

Tears accumulated and threatened to spill down her cheeks. He was being sincere after all. He truly was dying; this wasn't a bad dream. Mixed feelings rushed through her mind. First and foremost she felt a sense of loss, realizing that Derrick meant even more to her than she had recently come to realize. Against her better judgment, she had grown to love him. Was it a brotherly kind of love or a friendship type of love? It seemed more like a romantic love, but that made no sense at all. Whatever the case, losing someone she cared so deeply for would be devastating, and her feelings for him were strong and growing.

"Has a doctor actually told you that you're dying?"

He nodded.

"How long ago? When?"

Derrick hung his head and sniffed back tears. "Months ago."

At that moment Larissa understood all of the stress that Derrick had been under. "Wait a minute. How long after Sherry's death did you find out that you were dying?"

Derrick exhaled, the strain of the conversation registering on his face. "About a couple of weeks," he said.

Her eyes felt moist, her throat dry. "So within a span of two weeks you buried Sherry, then learned that your condition was terminal?"

Derrick nodded again.

"Oh my," she whispered with a hand over her chest. "Derrick . . ."

He obviously struggled to breathe.

"And then shortly after that, you met me," she said incredulously. "How on earth have you handled all of this so calmly? It seems impossible."

Swallowing hard, Derrick reminded her in a hoarse voice, "God never gives you more than you can handle."

Derrick's recent life was mind-boggling. Where did he get his strength to keep living despite all that had happened to him?

"I've only recently told Karen," he said.

"But what is it? There are treatments for everything."

He slowly massaged his forehead with his fingertips and in a low voice admitted, "I refused treatment. At the time I just wanted it to be over."

Feeling a spike of anger return, she leaned toward Derrick and said between gritted teeth, "Tell me that it wasn't for religious reasons that you refused treatment, that you didn't want to interfere with God's will."

"No . . . well, yes, to a small degree I didn't want to disrupt God's path for me," he answered, "but it was mainly my choice. I had been through so much with Sherry that my will to live was weak." He hung his head, then whispered, "God probably wasn't pleased with that, but it's all in the past now. I've been forgiven, and my conscience is clear."

Larissa felt her heart sink. How could this be happening? First Ken died, then she was falsely accused and arrested, she became a fugitive, then recently she lost Dixie. Why more? How was she supposed to handle one of the most special people in her life being taken away from her? Why would God do this to her?

Feeling a stronger surge of anger, Larissa squeezed his arm tighter than she intended. "You're *dying*, Derrick!" she screamed, then finished sarcastically, "So tell me something good *now!*"

Momentarily glancing away from her, Derrick paused, then turned back and looked her squarely in the eye. "I'm not dead yet," he whispered.

Rolling her eyes, Larissa wiped away tears and said, "You still haven't told me what it is."

Derrick cleared his throat and looked away. "I decided not to tell anyone. I didn't tell Karen either. I think it's best not to even talk about it."

"But why?"

He hesitated for a moment, then said, "Like I told her, I don't want you Googling miracle cures or home remedies. I don't want to be pitied. I want to live out my life as normally as possible without dwelling on it."

A cold silence hung between them. It dawned on Larissa that she had blamed God. She had to believe in Him to blame Him. That belief had been inspired by Derrick. This man had helped her see life from a whole new perspective. He had made her a better person, and now she had to let him go?

Larissa's eyes appeared red and swollen as she held back tears, and she leaned against him to deliver a huge hug. She began to shiver, then Derrick placed an arm around her and pulled her closer. "I'm sorry," she said between sobs. "I shouldn't have accused you of lying."

"It's okay," he assured her. "The rest of my days will be easier now that you know."

Her cries grew louder, her feelings stronger. She felt as if she were unraveling.

Derrick was in shock as he held her tight. It was strange how this moment of incredible sadness felt so good inside. He had never dreamed that Larissa would react this way. She obviously had feelings for him, strong ones, and she had no idea how wonderful and peaceful her embrace made him feel. If he had told her sooner, she may not have responded this way. He had only recently begun to sense a change in her, for the most part following Dixie's death, and now it was confirmed. He never could have imagined that dying could feel so good.

How crazy was this? They cared for each other under the most bizarre circumstances. He hoped her emotions were sincere. He had read years ago about something called Stockholm syndrome, wherein a kidnap victim develops feelings of dependence for the captor after an extended period of imprisonment. Could that possibly be the case here? No, it couldn't be. She hadn't been held against her will; she had been free to leave anytime she wanted, but perhaps this could be a variation of that condition. He would be devastated if her feelings were only artificial.

CHAPTER THIRTY-FIVE

Having adjusted to bringing the state of his health out into the open, Derrick and Larissa huddled together on the sofa a few days later, the iPad between them. He seemed stronger now, but Larissa knew that his improvement would only be temporary. His health would likely fluctuate from here on out.

"Before you check on the news, there's something I've been meaning to ask you. How did you come up with all those ideas to throw the cops off when we left Arizona?" Larissa asked.

"What do you mean?"

"Well, there's putting my DNA on the ski mask, pushing the driver's seat in my car back all the way, not to mention this whole cancer survivor disguise. It's really ingenious when I think about it. So how did you come up with all of those ideas?"

Derrick paused, looked away, then made eye contact again. "I didn't," he answered. A log in the fireplace shifted and dropped with a soft thud, sending sparks and flaming embers up through the chimney.

Baffled by such an unexpected response, Larissa asked through a puzzled expression, "What on earth does that mean?"

Derrick took a deep breath before looking back at her again. "Well, as we've discussed, all of this was meant to be, right?"

"So?"

"God put those ideas into my head. He had to; I'm not smart enough to come up with things like that on my own."

Larissa laughed. "Seriously, how did you do it?"

"I *am* being serious," Derrick countered. "Have you ever thought about where ideas come from?"

With a grin Larissa said sarcastically, "I can't say that I have."

"Well, I've thought about it a lot," he responded. "There have been plenty of times in my life that a thought hit me that was much too good for me to have come up with on my own. The only explanation is that God zapped the idea into my head."

With a light chuckle and a gentle shake of her head, Larissa had heard enough. She reached for the iPad and placed it on Derrick's lap. "Showtime," she said.

The familiar blonde reporter stood outside the Coconino Superior Court again, microphone in hand. "Coconino County District Attorney Wyatt Sanders's announcement today to drop all charges against Larissa Baxter came as no surprise to many who have been following the bizarre case," she said.

The video image cut to a press conference wherein a balding, short, out-of-shape man in his sixties appeared. Text at the bottom of the screen read *Wyatt Sanders, Coconino County District Attorney*.

"The nationwide manhunt for Larissa Baxter has been suspended and all charges against her have been dropped."

Someone off-screen asked, "Could she still be charged with unlawful flight to avoid prosecution?"

Sanders cleared his throat and answered, "Since she was technically under arrest at the time of her flight, the answer is yes, but that possibility has not yet been discussed."

Stock footage of the crime scene tape across the Baxter driveway appeared.

"Revelations of accused murderer Warren Pickett led investigators to re-examine evidence against Larissa Baxter as her husband's murderer. Her whereabouts remain unknown since she disappeared soon after posting bail."

Derrick turned to Larissa and smiled. "Congratulations!" he said, though the news was bittersweet.

She returned a weak grin and said, "Thanks. I've been praying about it."

"Praying?"

She raised her eyebrows, broadened her grin, but said nothing.

Derrick took a deep breath, then said, his voice weak, "I suppose this means you'll be going back to Arizona soon." He wondered if she detected the disappointment in his tone. No matter how hard he tried, he'd been unable to keep his emotions under control. He loved her unconditionally, even more so now that he knew she had feelings for him as well.

"I'm not sure . . ." she said hesitantly. "That last part of the statement concerns me. I wouldn't put it past the Baxters to push for my arrest for running away."

Now her grin disappeared, and her expression became sad. Her eyes grew wet as she said, "I'm not sure that I can leave you. Not after all we've been through and what still lies ahead."

Having never heard more beautiful words, Derrick smiled and marveled at her beauty. Her hair had grown to almost an inch and a half now, scraggly and misshapen, yet even under duress she appeared radiant, unlike he had seen her before. Would she actually consider staying with him till the end?

"This calls for a celebration," Larissa interrupted his thoughts.

"Absolutely. What do you have in mind?"

"Well . . ." She was obviously reluctant to say what she wanted. "I'd like to go out to dinner, dressed as the real me. No more disguises."

The very thought excited Derrick, but he wasn't quick to agree. Going out for a prolonged dinner would likely exhaust him, but he was reluctant to admit that to Larissa. Instead, he offered another excuse. "I'm not so sure. Do you think there's any way it could come back to haunt us?"

Larissa squeezed his shoulder and laughed. "Sometimes you're just way too over-protective. Let's throw caution to the wind, okay?"

How could he resist? It would be wonderful to see her relaxed and comfortable, something he had yet to experience. He even imagined what a thrill it would be to have a real date with such a bombshell beauty. Of course, most would assume that she was his daughter, and some might presume that such a gorgeous woman in the company of a much older man could only be a high-price hooker, but if people who knew him saw them together, they would be totally perplexed. He would smile from ear to ear and simply introduce her as Sarah without any explanation of her connection to him. It was nobody's business anyway.

A quick glance at the fireplace reminded Derrick that he fortunately had amassed a rather large stockpile of firewood as his ability to swing an axe was now severely limited. He had to take advantage of every opportunity while he still physically could, so why not push himself to comply with Larissa's wishes?

She cast a mischievous look his way with a questioning glance. "Let's do it!" he exclaimed.

He had hoped to take her to his favorite local restaurant, Stemley Station, but remembered that Karen had told him it had burned to the ground while he was in Arizona. Larissa deserved a good meal at a nice place, and there were decent eateries in nearby Pell City and Talladega, but, feeling weaker by the minute, Derrick honestly didn't think he had enough energy for a long, drawn-out, sit-down meal and hoped she would be satisfied with The Shack. It was nearby, fast, and unique, after all.

Larissa was stunning in tight jeans and a low-cut top as she slid into the Tahoe's passenger seat. Even Walmart looked great on her. "Derrick?" she said. He jarred himself to attention as she said, "You're staring."

Derrick blushed, cleared this throat, and turned on the ignition. "Get used to it," he said. "Every man who sees you tonight will do the same. Don't you think you should wear something a bit more . . . loose?"

Larissa laughed and patted him on the knee. "Come on, cowboy, let's live a little."

She agreed that The Shack would be a good destination. She'd been curious about it anyway. They sat at a table near the back, close to where he had met Karen previously. Larissa marveled at the hewn log walls and rustic decor. Derrick had never seen her so relaxed, laughing and smiling. Of course, she had a reason to; she had a whole new life ahead of her. She'd been totally vindicated, and there was no way she could be charged for fleeing prosecution without a countercharge for false arrest. For her own benefit, however, the end of her story would play out better on her own terms without her being spotted by someone and forced to reveal herself prematurely. She still needed to maintain the upper hand, although she didn't seem to realize it.

As he put an end to his barbecue sandwich and fries, Larissa locked eyes with him from across the table, and he swore she bore the expression of a woman in love. His heart swelled with joy. Being with her this way was like experiencing ten Christmases all at once.

"My life has been crazy since I met you," she said, following a sip of iced tea, "but mostly in a good way." She dabbed her lips with a napkin and maintained steady eye contact.

Derrick was at a loss for words. For the first time since their paths had crossed he felt insecure and tongue-tied with a lump in his throat at being in her presence in a purely social environment.

"I don't mean to embarrass you," she said. "I just feel so alive after hiding for so long. It's like I can finally breathe again."

From the corner of his eye, Derrick noticed two men at a nearby table staring at Larissa. They appeared to be hatching a plan to approach her. Didn't they see that she was with someone? Did he truly fear that she would be identified or was this only a touch of jealousy? Realistically, however, he probably looked more like her father than a date.

At first he swelled with pride that other men would envy him being out with a beautiful woman, but after realizing that it was a sinful reaction on his part, his protective instinct kicked back in again, and he wanted to get her out of there. His energy slowly dissipating, his pulse quickened. "Hey . . ." he said in a low whisper, "let's get out of here."

"But—"

"Come on," he insisted, throwing enough cash onto the table to cover the check and a generous tip.

As they passed the two men, he heard one of them push back on his chair and start to say something, but Derrick tugged Larissa along and whisked her out the door. At the Tahoe he gasped to catch his breath, noticing Larissa slam the passenger door when she slid inside. She refused to look at him as he approached the right turn at Handy Corner.

"Larissa . . . I'm sorry," he apologized. "I shouldn't . . . have overreacted that way."

She maintained her stance, avoiding eye contact.

"But . . . they were staring . . . at you," he pleaded. Taking a deep breath, he grasped the steering wheel tighter as he thought of a way to get his point across. "I know that you've . . . been cleared," he continued, "but you need to . . . keep control of . . . your situation. Don't let . . . unforeseen circumstances force you to . . . call your own hand. Do it on your own terms . . . when you're ready." He paused, trying to gauge her reaction. She seemed to be softening a bit. "After all . . . you've been through . . . I just want things . . . to work out for you . . . the best way possible."

She was miffed but still beautiful. Derrick knew that he faced even more challenges now as Larissa ventured into the public and attracted male attention. He'd never been the jealous type and couldn't understand the hold she had over him.

CHAPTER THIRTY-SIX

Larissa's over-confidence from recent developments in Flagstaff was a growing concern for Derrick. Since their celebration dinner out, she'd been more careless about protecting her identity and more determined than ever to have a public life again. He knew that she shouldn't reveal herself to the world yet and preferred her to be more cautious, although his degree of concern only disguised his real reason for wanting to stay at home. Simple activity like a mere walk to the Tahoe in the driveway tired him now, and he finally admitted to himself that he may not be able to venture out many more times.

Derrick was annoyed at her now because she had insisted on a quick run to Walmart and was dressed to kill once again, wearing the skin-tight jeans she'd purchased on their last discreet shopping trip and more makeup than their recent night out. He thought she looked much better without it. She was far too striking and would attract undue attention. Still, it was her life, so Derrick gave in after voicing his objection.

At the Pell City Walmart Derrick noticed more than one man captivated by Larissa's looks. Each time she bent over or reached up for something, her jeans and blouse hugged her even tighter and drew more stares.

On the way home he couldn't help but express himself. "I don't understand you . . . sometimes," he started the conversation, unsure if he had enough energy for a confrontational discussion.

"What do you mean?" she answered.

Derrick groaned. "Well," he said, "you're not helping yourself by . . . by dressing the way you do." It had become more difficult to say complete sentences without pausing for a deep breath.

With a huff she answered, "Derrick, we've been over this. I've got to be myself. I'm tired of hiding behind a mask, and if someone identifies me, well . . . maybe that's meant to be."

Derrick slowly shook his head. "Please don't use . . . that kind of reasoning. God gave you . . . a brain to keep you out of . . . trouble."

Larissa shrugged. "So if someone exposes me, I'll cross that bridge when I come to it."

Derrick gave a sarcastic laugh. "You'll deal with it . . . then?" he said in amazement. "And just how will you . . . deal with being publicly exposed . . . unexpectedly? Have you . . . given any thought . . . to all of the attention . . . to the cameras and microphones shoved at your face . . . the uncomfortable questions . . . the media will throw at you?"

She silently stared ahead as the windshield wipers swept away a few raindrops.

"How will you . . . explain where you've been . . . the past several months?"

He knew that she was ignoring him but proceeded anyway. "I warned you that men would . . . stare at you, and that's exactly . . . what happened. Your face has been . . . plastered across the news again since the charges . . . were dropped." He grew more exhausted by the minute.

The anger in her voice was more than obvious. "You act like I'm some kind of goddess, Derrick, like I'm a glamour queen in a spotlight. I'm just a thirtysomething-year-old woman who's past her prime and wants to look decent when she goes out. There's no harm in that."

Derrick felt exasperated. Past her prime? Who was she kidding? "That guy couldn't take . . . his eyes off you. Was it because he recognized you . . . from news reports or because of . . . those tight pants? We'll never . . . know for sure unless . . . we get a knock on the door tonight . . . from a cop or a news reporter."

Larissa placed her left hand on Derrick's right knee and squeezed. "I appreciate your concern for me, I really do, but I have to admit it felt good to be noticed again." Her tone had softened.

Turning right at Handy Corner, Derrick wasn't sure what she had meant by that. Was she inferring that he hadn't shown her enough attention or that she simply missed the adulation of men that she'd been accustomed to her entire life?

"Derrick?" she broke the silence. "How are you feeling? I can tell you're struggling to even keep up a conversation."

He grimaced and said, "Don't try to . . . change the subject." He grasped the steering wheel tighter and gritted his teeth. "Okay, okay," he said. "Forgive me for being . . . concerned."

They rode the rest of the way home in silence.

CHAPTER THIRTY-SEVEN

By the time they turned down the steep driveway, Larissa knew that Derrick couldn't have driven much farther. As he brought the Tahoe to a stop outside the house, he switched off the ignition and collapsed against the back of the seat trying to catch his breath. Finally, he reached down and pulled the door lever. When he started to push the door open, Larissa said, "Wait. Let me help you!"

He didn't object. Larissa raced around the car to the driver's door and started to pull him out. How could he have possibly gotten so much worse in such a short period of time? He leaned against her, and it almost felt like transporting dead weight. Slowly they made their way to the door and, once inside, she led him to his bedroom. Derrick collapsed onto the bed, still breathing heavily.

Larissa sat on the mattress beside him and lightly shook him; he seemed only semi-conscious. Taking out her cell phone, she said, "I've got to call for help."

He groaned and gripped her wrist weakly. "No . . . please . . . don't."

"But, Derrick, I can't do anything for you. EMTs can treat you and get you to a hospital. I can't just watch you suffer like this."

He swallowed hard, then pleaded, "No . . . I want to be here . . . with you."

Larissa began to sob. She stripped him down to his underwear so he would be more comfortable. "I don't like this, Derrick. This isn't—"

Her words were interrupted by the buzzing vibration of a cell phone. It wasn't hers. She immediately realized it was Derrick's, in his pocket where she had placed his pants on the dresser. She slipped it out and answered, "Hello?"

"I know you guys must have heard the big news already," Karen said excitedly, "so why haven't you called—wait a minute; Larissa? Why are you answering Derrick's phone?"

Larissa softly sobbed, trying to regain her composure.

"Larissa? Are you . . . crying?"

Larissa took a deep breath, then said, "Karen . . . he's taken a bad turn. You need to get over here."

"I'm on my way," Karen said and disconnected the call.

Larissa turned back to Derrick. His eyes were only half open. She felt his forehead, but he had no fever. Instead, he felt cool and clammy.

"Derrick?" she prodded him. He was unresponsive.

She looked him up and down, then said, "I don't care what you say, I'm getting help."

With a weak, shaky hand he reached out for her. "No . . . hospital," he begged, his voice barely above a whisper. "I . . . don't want . . . to . . . miss a minute . . . inside this house . . . with you."

Maybe Karen could help convince him. Larissa knew she couldn't get medical help for him if he refused it. She patted his chest, leaned over, and kissed his forehead. "Try to get some rest," she said softly. "Karen's on her way."

Clearing his voice, Derrick spoke in a hoarse, raspy tone. "Tell me . . . something good," he said.

Sniffling with a lingering smile, Larissa promptly answered, "That's a no brainer. I'm here with you."

After a brief fit of coughing and groaning subsided, Derrick struggled with the words but finally got them out. "That's what . . . I was going to say."

Larissa went to the living room, sat on the cream-colored sofa, and felt as if her world was coming to an end. Her heart pounded, her vision blurred from mounting tears. She hadn't expected such a sudden decline for Derrick. She had assumed there would be more memorable times ahead on the deck, sitting on the pier, feeling the warmth of the fireplace together, his health only deteriorating gradually.

Her mind raced back to the moment she learned that Ken had been shot. What a bizarre life she had led since. It was stranger than fiction, yet here she was, far from home, caring for a dying man whom she had only known a short while but loved so dearly.

By the time Karen arrived, Larissa had calmed somewhat. *I've got to be strong,* she reminded herself. Karen was now at Derrick's bedside. His voice had grown somewhat stronger, and he insisted on speaking with his sister alone. They had been in his room with the door closed for almost an hour. Larissa listened as Karen's raised but muffled voice grew louder at times separated by bursts of crying. Perhaps Karen's attempt to convince Derrick that he needed medical attention was no more successful than her own. Regardless, Larissa felt her own level of anxiety rising. She wished she could get medication for her own growing stress, but there was simply no way.

She stepped to the window and stared across the water. Moonlight reflected off ripples in the lake, and the brightest stars speckled the sky. Larissa closed her eyes and began to pray. It was still something new for her, and she felt uncomfortable at first, but as she silently mouthed the words, a rush of emotion overcame her and calmed her. She realized that everything would be alright in the long run. Derrick was going to a better place, pain-free and strong, and she herself would be better off, too, leading a spiritually-based life.

When she opened her eyes, Larissa felt that God had, indeed, touched her and given her strength. She smiled, then reminded herself that God was another of the many things that Derrick had brought into her life.

Finally, Karen exited the bedroom and quietly closed the door behind her. Larissa looked up through the cedar railing and their eyes met, then Karen came downstairs to join her on the sofa. She took Larissa's hand and said between sobs, "I never expected it to be like this, for him to grow worse so quickly."

Larissa squeezed Karen's hand and asked, "Did you convince him to get help?"

Karen shook her head. "He's been quirky all his life. As much as I don't like it, it doesn't surprise me that he refuses help."

"Oh no," Larissa said and hung her head.

"And it shouldn't have surprised me that he won't tell us what's killing him. I reckon it's a typical Derrickthing to do."

Larissa leaned over and hugged Karen. "I feel like I'm falling apart," she whispered into Karen's ear.

Karen returned her embrace and offered, "Well, try to focus on the good news from Flagstaff for a while and get your mind off Derrick. You need the rest."

Larissa was confused. "More news?" she asked. "I thought I had heard the end of it."

"Oh my," Karen began. "They've made an arrest. The real killer is behind bars."

The news was difficult to absorb. Of course it would have a tremendous impact on her future, but at the moment that was the least of her concerns. Her immediate worry was Derrick, and she would stay by his side until the very end.

CHAPTER THIRTY-EIGHT

For several days Derrick's condition fluctuated. Most days were bad, but a few decent moments occurred here and there. Larissa cared for his every need, feeding him when necessary and bathing him, all modesty lost. She did everything possible to keep him comfortable. Occasionally he was able to talk, albeit slowly, and she cherished every conversation, however brief.

Today Larissa eyed him up and down as he slept, noting how drastically his appearance had changed since they first met. As she was about to leave his room, Derrick coughed and opened his eyes. He looked at her with one of the saddest expressions she'd ever seen and said, "I'm . . . sorry."

She stood motionless, staring at him dumbfounded, then finally asked, "Whatever for?" thrilled that perhaps she might have at least a limited talk with him.

Derrick breathed hard and answered, "For . . . all . . . of this."

She stepped back to his bedside and sat next to him. "Do you mean for me taking care of you?"

He gave a slight nod, which she knew was difficult for him.

"Derrick . . ." she began, "I'm here because I want to be."

"But—"

"No, listen to me. Derrick, they've arrested someone for Ken's murder. I'm totally free. I could go anywhere now, but I choose to be *here* . . . with *you*."

His expression changed, and he obviously tried to smile. He seemed as happy as someone in his condition could possibly be. Larissa stroked his thinning hair with her fingertips and leaned closer.

"Derrick, you scared me to death when you came at me from out of nowhere in my garage wearing a mask. Looking back, I was probably crazy to have gone on the run with you, but there was something in your eyes that made me trust you."

A slight smile appeared on his face and stuck.

"I've learned a lot from you," she continued. "I feel like I've grown in so many ways." Tears ran down her cheeks. "You told me once that the reason you saved me was because you needed to do something good to atone for your sins."

Tears ran from Derrick's eyes as well.

"But that's crazy, Derrick. Since those conversations I've learned that you've been a good man all your life. You didn't have to prove anything to yourself or anyone else." She sniffled as her emotions overcame her. "How you cared for your wife after she . . . I just can't comprehend how someone could be so forgiving and loving."

Larissa leaned over to hug him, but he was unable to reciprocate, so she held him tight and cried. Derrick quietly sobbed as well. Several minutes passed before she was able to speak again. "I'll be with you every moment," she said between sobs. "Nothing could drive me away."

She saw the happiness in his eyes and felt overwhelmed by the commanding emotions flowing throughout her body.

"I—I—"

Larissa placed her index finger over his lips and shushed him. "Don't use up your energy. The next time I'll let you do all the talking." She pulled the covers up to his chin and tucked him in. "Get some rest. I'll see your smiling face again in the morning."

Derrick's eyes slowly closed as she stepped to the door and turned out the light. Larissa felt a rare warmth inside. The torch had been passed. Derrick had been there for her in her moment of greatest need, and now he was the one in peril.

***

A few days later, after Karen had visited Derrick again, she asked Larissa if they could talk. Larissa brewed a pot of coffee, and the two sat in the living room. Karen took a sip, exhaled, then said, "I don't know how you're holding up. You must be worn slap out. Caring for him now is a twenty-four-seven job, and you shouldn't feel so obligated."

Larissa took a drink and set her cup on the coffee table. "There's nothing I'd rather be doing," she said.

"But Larissa," Karen continued, "you're free to do anything you want now. You can start your life over and be as free as a bird. I can take care of him now."

Larissa didn't like where this conversation was going. "Look," she said, "your brother and I have admittedly had one of the strangest relationships I've ever heard of, and I certainly don't expect you to understand, but this is where I want to be, where I *need* to be."

Karen took another sip and sighed. "I knew you would say that, so here's what I think. You need help; this is way too much for one person to handle. Either I should stay here until the end or I can have Derrick moved to my house. You're welcome to come, too. It's a big house, and we've got plenty of room. Either way, you and I can take better care of him together."

Larissa massaged her forehead with her fingertips, then looked Karen in the eye. "Moving him away from here is out of the question. He's made it clear over and over that he wants to spend every moment in this house."

"That comes as no surprise either," Karen said.

An awkward silence hung between them until Karen added, "Then how about me staying here? It's your call."

Larissa carefully considered the offer. She could absolutely use the help, but it would come at a cost. She firmly believed that Derrick wouldn't be as relaxed and comfortable if Karen were there. "That's awfully kind of you," she finally said, "and I know how much you love your brother, and he loves you, too. Let's give it a few more days, then you'll be welcome to—"

Larissa stopped abruptly, embarrassed.

"What's wrong?" Karen asked. "Are you feeling okay?"

"Yes . . . It just occurred to me that I have no right to decide who stays in this house and who doesn't. I'm not related to Derrick, and I don't own this house. You're his family; you should be making all the decisions, not me."

Karen placed a hand over Larissa's, which rested atop her knee. "You said it yourself," Karen began. "You and Derrick have a crazy relationship that no one can possibly understand. I know he loves you and that he wants you to be in charge. I'm just offering some help, that's all. I only want to honor his wishes."

A smile crossed Larissa's face for the first time in days. The mood felt right again. "Thank you, Karen," she said. "You just keep visiting him every day, and I'll let you know when the time is right for you to move in."

Karen paused in obvious deep thought before finally saying, "I can't help but wonder how this would all be playing out now if Sherry were still alive. You're so much more compassionate and attentive to him than she ever would have been."

Larissa smiled, feeling good about herself but also recognizing how sad it was that a woman who had been married to Derrick for so long wasn't held in higher regard by his sister.

After exchanging a few more pleasantries, Karen left and Larissa was again virtually alone in a dark, silent house.

CHAPTER THIRTY-NINE

A heavy pall hung over the Walton household. Day after day Larissa checked on Derrick regularly; sometimes he was awake, but more often he was not. He just lay there motionless in his bed, barely breathing, his complexion pale, almost wax-like in appearance, and his breathing became more labored minute by minute.

Nights seemed far worse than days. The house lay eerily quiet except for the creaking staircase, and Larissa felt incredibly alone. She had reluctantly decided that tomorrow she would tell Karen it was time for her to move in. It would drastically change the household dynamics, but with Derrick more asleep than conscious, he probably wouldn't even realize that his sister was sleeping under the same roof. Karen had been a nurse's aid at one time, and her additional care would definitely be in Derrick's best interest. Without a doubt Larissa knew that she and Karen, together, could care for Derrick's every need.

Shortly after 9:00 p.m. Larissa showered and readied herself for bed. One more check on Derrick and she would retire for the evening. In the dim night light of the room she saw his eyes were half open, so she stepped to his side and squeezed his hand. He returned a light grasp, the first indication in days that he knew she was there, and Larissa became flooded with emotion when he winced in obvious pain.

Tears spilled from her eyes. She opened the overhead curtains to allow moonlight in, stroked his head, and ran her fingertips tenderly down his cheeks. She watched his Adam's apple barely move up and down almost in slow motion. Memories flashed through her mind as she recalled how he'd once said that she couldn't "ugly herself up" if she tried. Larissa closed her eyes, thinking about that night in her garage. No matter how hard Derrick tried, he couldn't make himself appear to be a bad guy either. He had to have been the most inept kidnapper ever.

He'd cared for her every step of the way, had put everything at risk to protect her, and had been a gentleman every moment. Oh, she'd noticed how he had looked at her at times. He was a man, after all. He lay clinging to life now, and Larissa would bet that, if he was lucid, he was thinking about her at that very moment. This sweet, sweet man would soon be gone, and she wasn't sure how she would handle the loss.

Without thinking, Larissa rolled the bed sheet down and crawled into the bed beside him, turning to face him with an arm around his chest.

Derrick's breath quickened; he apparently sensed her presence. There was so much she wanted to say, yet she was too choked up with emotion to get the words out, so she had to just lie there and tenderly caress his face and shoulders for a moment. A slight chill hung in the air, so she pulled the sheet up to cover them.

"Derrick," she began. "I hope you can hear me."

He gave no response.

"I can't let you go without telling you . . . what you've meant to me." She stopped to sniffle and took a deep breath. "You saved me when I didn't want to be saved. You changed me when I didn't want to be changed. You made a new woman out of me, but I know this is the way I should have been all along."

Tears clouded her vision, and she thought she saw the semblance of a smile, a glimmer of awareness, but couldn't be sure. "Derrick . . . It can't be just a coincidence that I'm here with you now. This was meant to be. I know I was hard-headed and stubborn about it, but you were right. This has been our destiny."

She felt his hand lightly graze against her hip, and her crying intensified. "I want you to rest now, Derrick. You're weak, so don't try to say anything. I just want you to know that . . . I love you . . . and my love for you trumps all other feelings that I've ever had, the only way it should be. I totally understand now why you stuck by Sherry regardless of what she did to you. It was your love for her that mattered, not her lack of feelings for you."

She placed her index finger at his lips to prevent him from speaking. There was nothing he could say anyway; he had said it all before. She only wanted him to rest while she slept beside him.

"God," she whispered softly, "please ease Derrick's pain and give him comfort." She stopped to sniffle, then continued, "He's given me faith in you and faith in life again. I hope you have a special place for him."

Larissa snuggled closer and silently prayed that Derrick had heard her confession of love.

His mind was a series of undulating waves without clarity. He heard sounds fading in and out like the poor reception of a distant radio station. He couldn't open his eyes.

Was Larissa with him now? He could barely move his hands, but . . . he felt her breath against his ear. Slowly his sense of touch awakened, and he felt the warmth of her embrace. He smelled her freshly shampooed hair and wanted to hold her but couldn't. He had no energy left at all. The realization was agonizing at first, but then he knew that he should be thankful that she was expressing herself this way.

Hearing her precious words, he felt tears pool in his almost lifeless eyes, then gently roll down his cheeks. Nothing in his entire life compared to this moment. Derrick's pulse slowed, his eyelids grew heavy. He was at peace with himself more than at any time in his life.

The sounds inside his head grew in clarity, and the echoing barks of a dog had to be Dixie waiting for him. This had to be the first step on the stairway to heaven . . .

***

Still lying closely beside him, Larissa was awakened early by stray dogs barking outside, probably those that had attacked her. A cold chill suddenly ran down her body. She couldn't hear even a whisper of breath from Derrick. Touching his cheeks, his chest, she felt nothing but cold. Lifeless. She shook him but got no response. He had passed sometime during the night.

Larissa cried like never before. Grief poured from her in waves. She had lost a husband to murder, but her sorrow then was only a fraction of what she felt now. She knew that she needed to call Karen but didn't feel she could speak coherently yet.

Slowly she eased from the bed. All she could think of was what a horrible, horrible loss she, and the world, had just suffered.

Fleeting memories again ran through her mind, of her screaming at Derrick to get the dead fish off the deck, having deep spiritual discussions that eventually erased any doubt in her faith. She thought of him again as a cowboy in a western romance, her knight in shining armor, and he'd unselfishly wanted nothing more than to give her a second chance at life.

And that he had.

Talladega County, Alabama

One week later

Nothing was the same; the house, the view, the silence. It was as if a 3-D movie had suddenly turned black and white and one-dimensional. Derrick's funeral service had been held the day before, and Larissa packed the few things she had accumulated and was prepared to leave soon—for where she had not yet decided. Awaiting Karen's arrival to scatter his ashes into the lake at the end of the pier, she took a moment to relax on the sofa with Derrick's iPad.

She couldn't remember the last time she checked on developments back home and was pleased that her story had been reduced to a minor "Continuing News" header on a Flagstaff television station. Amused at the video report's title, "*Where Is Larissa Baxter?*" she clicked on a link for the report to begin.

A slightly plump Hispanic female reporter held a microphone while standing in Larissa's driveway, where a few remaining tattered strands of yellow crime scene tape still streamed in the wind.

"With the arrest and arraignment of Hank Spyker for the murder of real estate developer Kenneth Baxter, the question on everyone's mind remains: Where is Larissa Baxter?" the reporter announced. "Having been completely exonerated for any involvement in the crime, Mrs. Baxter, who presumably fled from prosecution while released on bail, has been expected to resurface. I spoke with Mrs. Baxter's defense attorney, Harvey Bateman, who had this to say."

The scene cut to Bateman's office, where he sat behind a massive walnut desk with packed bookcases behind him.

"I've been adamant from the beginning that Mrs. Baxter did not leave voluntarily, but was in fact kidnapped," Bateman began. "I'm appalled that authorities never took her possible abduction seriously when evidence at the crime scene, including her DNA on the kidnapper's ski mask, suggested that she was taken by force."

The reporter interjected, "What would you like to say to Mrs. Baxter, assuming she can hear you?"

Bateman cleared his throat and stated, "Larissa, the legal system has let you down in many ways, not only by falsely arresting you in the first place, but also by failing to protect you and not searching for you as a victim rather than a fugitive. I pray that you'll be home soon."

Switching back to the reporter, the news clip finished with: "Not everyone agrees with Bateman's assessment. Rumors continue to fly that Mrs. Baxter was indeed involved in the murder of her husband and now resides under an assumed identity with a lover. Some believe that she has committed suicide while others are firm in their belief that she has died at the hands of a sexual predator.

"If she fails to surface soon, Larissa Baxter could prove to be the twenty-first century's version of famed robber and parachute escapist D. B. Cooper, who jumped from a plane in 1971 and has never been seen since."

Larissa couldn't help but smile at the thought of being such a mystery woman back home. She would give serious thought to living a life of seclusion to keep them guessing. It wouldn't hurt to try; at least it was something to consider.

It had only been a fleeting thought before an emptiness inside overcame her again. Despite the moment of diversion, it left her stunned and drained. Absorbing the developments in her life over the last several months had been more than overwhelming.

Staring out the window from the sofa, she then glanced back at the empty fireplace where the embers had died when Derrick's health had rapidly declined. Once Karen's car came to a stop in the driveway, Larissa heard the door of her car slam shut. For the first time since she'd lived in this house, she realized that no one would greet Karen at the door. Derrick and Dixie were no longer there to do it, and Larissa simply wasn't up to it.

Moments later a light rap at the door sounded. When Larissa opened it, a gust of cold wind blasted past Karen and into the house. Quickly closing the door behind her, Karen reached to Larissa for an embrace. No words were spoken. The two women clung to each other and cried, holding on to one another as if their lives depended on it. As they began to regain their composure, Larissa finally said, "I think we need to sit down."

Karen shrugged out of her coat and followed Larissa to the living room. Neither was in the mood for refreshments. Larissa knew that she must look a mess with her puffy, swollen eyes and no makeup, and for the first time in her life she didn't care.

"I miss him," Karen said. "He always made me laugh when we were kids, but he could be mean as a snake, too. Sometimes he was just too big for his britches."

Larissa had been unnerved by the stillness of the house, and the quiet was enough to drive her crazy. It was nice to hear someone else's voice. She glanced at the urn on the mantel. "He was so much a part of this place," she said. "I've never known anyone so connected to his home. He was as vital to this house as the roof or the foundation." She sobbed louder now, wiping tears from her cheeks. "I've never met anyone so passionate about his heritage and where he lived."

"I couldn't agree with you more," Karen said as she touched Larissa's arm.

"But he had to go and get himself mixed up with me. He broke the law and was stuck in hiding with me when he could have enjoyed his final days in this wonderful place without the stress I caused him."

Karen touched Larissa's hand that still twitched and shook atop her knee. "He wouldn't have wanted it any other way," she said.

Larissa took a deep breath. "Should we go outside and set Derrick free now?" she suggested.

Karen cleared her throat. "Not just yet," she said. "We need to talk first."

Larissa was puzzled, but curious. What left could there be to say?

Karen removed Derrick's silver cross and chain from her purse. "He wanted you to have this," she said.

Stunned, Larissa felt her emotions overwhelm her. Never had the sight of an object of any kind affected her this way. She reached out, took the medallion, and squeezed it. In a flash she recalled the confrontation in her garage and realized that it was this simple crucifix that had first caught her attention, not the gun, not the ski mask. It had to have been a message from God, yet she hadn't realized it till now. "Oh!" she exclaimed. Her hand shook as she examined the cross more closely. "I can't believe Derrick knew how much this would mean to me. Thank you so much!"

With a smile Karen whispered, "There's more" as she took two business-size white envelopes from her purse and set them on her lap, then squeezed Larissa's hand again.

"When I came to visit Derrick that first time after he took a turn for the worse, he wanted to speak to me privately, remember?"

"Yes, of course," Larissa said. "And?"

Karen cleared her throat again, hesitating briefly, then said, "He wanted to be sure that you would be taken care of . . . after he was gone."

"He never mentioned anything about that to me," Larissa responded.

Karen nodded. "Derrick was a private man in many ways. Anyway, in all honesty, I tried to talk him out of it. I didn't think he was in his right mind. I had the only copy of his existing will, which was done after Sherry's death. It had all the bells and whistles to pass as a legal document, and I knew that producing a new will at that late stage of his life would've been extremely difficult. It would've required several witnesses to attest to his signature and that sort of thing, and I wasn't even sure at that point if he could even physically sign it himself, but I didn't tell him that. I didn't want to upset him, so I just listened and played along."

Larissa was astonished that Derrick had thought of leaving her anything at all in his will, and it wasn't something that she felt strongly about. Derrick was a modest man of modest means, however, so perhaps he had wanted her to have something else of sentimental value.

"When I left Derrick that night, I didn't intend to follow through with his wishes," Karen continued. "Again, I thought he wasn't in his right mind and didn't know what he was saying." She handed one of the white envelopes to Larissa. "This is his last legal will. He was leaving everything to me."

Larissa found it interesting that Karen was making such a production about it. Leaving everything to a loving sister had been the practical thing to do, but what could she, Larissa, have to do with it?

"But as I watched you taking care of him since that day, my conscience began to bother me," Karen went on. "I knew how much he loved you, and it became obvious that you felt something similar for him. You were there by his side every moment as if you had spent your entire life with him. I've never seen anything like it. Sherry never showed him even half of the concern that you did."

Larissa slowly shook her head and interjected, "Let me stop you for just a minute. None of this matters to me, Karen. I took care of Derrick because it was the right thing to do. No one else ever impacted my life the way he did, so I wanted to give him all of the help that I could. It was totally a labor of love, and I never expected anything in return."

Karen nodded. "I know that now. In a strange way you were the best thing that ever happened to Derrick. You gave him a purpose in life at a time when he needed it most, when he felt lost and didn't know what to do with himself. You gave him peace and happiness when he knew his days were numbered. You gave him someone to love, and love was always hugely important to him." She paused a moment, then added, "You've become like family to me, and I don't want you to move away."

Larissa's vision became distorted by tears, her emotions getting the best of her again. She missed him so much and knew there would never be anyone else quite like him in her life.

Karen was obviously trying to compose herself. This conversation was apparently difficult for her. She handed Larissa the other envelope.

"I created this document on my computer. I entered everything from his original will, then modified it to reflect his dying wishes." She paused to wipe tears from her own eyes. "There's nothing legal about it. It doesn't have his signature and, of course, no witnesses."

Larissa still listened intently. "He wanted you to have this house, Larissa. He paid off the mortgage years ago, so it's all free and clear. You can't possibly realize what this house meant to him or how much you—"

"Oh, but I do," Larissa interrupted. She was shocked by the magnitude of his intentions, whether they were ever realized or not. "This house was a part of him. It's almost as if this place died with him. It's just not the same without him, and it never will be."

Karen shook her head and countered, "I'm not sure that I would agree with that. Derrick thought you could maintain the spirit of the house that he cherished so much. He told me that over and over. He was convinced that you belong here."

"But what about you?" Larissa asked. "This should be your house. You're his next of kin."

"Don't think that he didn't consider my feelings. He asked me several times that night if I would be okay with it. He wanted to make sure that I didn't feel slighted. I told him it would be no problem for me. At the time I was just playing along; anything to make him feel better."

Larissa sniffled and wiped her tears. "I understand how you reacted then, but how do you feel now? You've had a lot of pleasant memories in this house, too."

With a laugh Karen said, "You're right. I've had many happy times here. But I have a feeling that if you live here, you won't mind me dropping by from time to time."

Again, Larissa realized how much in life she'd missed by not having a sibling to love. "You were a devoted sister to him, and I know how much he loved you," she said, "and of course you would always be welcomed here, but it doesn't matter anyway since it's not legal, and I wouldn't accept it anyway."

Karen shifted on the sofa and gazed at the cedar walls of the living room. She took a deep breath, then looked Larissa in the eye. "This is what Derrick wanted," she said, pointing to the second envelope. "I can forge his signature. I have friends who would sign it as witnesses without even knowing what the document is. They trust me. I can make Derrick's last will stand up legally, which wouldn't be difficult because there will be no one to contest it anyway. I can get the deed transferred to you."

Larissa stared blankly at Karen and said, "I don't know what to say." She paused, then added, "Well, I do know this. I would never want nor expect you to do that. It just doesn't feel right. Besides, my life isn't here. My life is . . . well, I'm not quite sure where my life is anymore, but I don't think it's here."

"Don't be so quick to say that," Karen pointed out. "You've seemed mighty comfortable here to me." She stood from the sofa and turned in a circle, gazing at every corner of the room. "I know this house doesn't seem like much to you after the way you lived in Arizona, but it was Derrick's heart and soul. You were his heart and soul, too, Larissa. Just think about it. You've got both versions of his will, and all I ask is that you consider what Derrick wanted."

Larissa set the envelopes on the coffee table and stood. "I need some fresh air," she said.

As Larissa stepped to the armoire to grab a light jacket, Karen remained seated. "Don't you think it's too cold to sit outside?" she asked.

Without hesitation Larissa answered, "It's not that bad. It just feels too stuffy in here."

Slipping on her coat, Karen followed, taking the urn from the mantel with her.

Outside on the deck, Larissa did feel a bit chilly, but she could definitely breathe better. A stiff breeze blew across her face and ruffled her lengthening hair. She took a deep breath and listened to the peaceful sound of waves lapping against the shore and the rusty hinges of the floating section of pier squeak as Karen set the urn on the picnic table and joined her, making a shivering sound.

"I'll miss this place," Larissa said, "and I'll never forget it either. It's been almost like a fairy tale to me."

Before Karen could respond, they both heard a whining sound coming from below the deck. "What on earth is that?" Karen asked.

They stepped off the deck and rounded the corner to investigate. Far in the back corner underneath the deck, huddled against the concrete block foundation wall of the house, a small, frightened, shivering brown and white puppy lay. "Oh, you poor thing," Karen said. "People abandon animals around here all the time. It's so disgusting."

Larissa knelt and called to the dog in a soothing voice, motioning for it to come to her. Slowly, shaking from head to toe, the pup reluctantly made its way toward her, its tail starting to wag slightly as it approached. As she patted the dog's back, it became playful and bounced on its feet in front of Larissa. "You must be a dog lover," Karen said. "Dogs can sense it."

Larissa picked up the mutt and checked its gender, then set it back on the ground. "Come on, boy," she said. "Let's get you something to eat."

They returned to the top of the deck, and Larissa went inside to the kitchen. Dixie's dish and half a bag of dry food were still underneath the sink. With food and water in hand, she stepped back onto the deck and watched the dog devour and drink nonstop. The two women sat at the picnic table silently for a few moments, watching the dog and taking in the scenery.

Larissa took the urn from the picnic table, stared at the pier, and said, "Let's do this before we freeze."

They silently walked the urn to the end of the pier. A frigid breeze swept Larissa's hair, and she began to shudder. Karen turned to Larissa, her own hair in her face, and said, "I can almost sense his presence." Larissa handed the urn to Karen, who said, "I'd like to say a short prayer if you don't mind."

"Of course," Larissa almost whispered in a shivering voice past the lump in her throat.

The floating pier rocked gently. They bowed their heads, and Karen prayed, holding the urn tight against her chest. "Heavenly Father, we return the ashes of our brother and special friend for your eternal care. He was one your finest creations, a man who served you and the people he loved with undying devotion. I know you're as proud of him as we are. In Jesus's name we pray. Amen."

Larissa opened her eyes. "That was a sweet prayer, but don't tell me you made it up at the spur of the moment."

Karen laughed between chattering teeth. "No, I sort of composed it in my mind on the way over here," she responded. Karen obviously struggled to hold back tears. "Would you like to say something?" she asked.

Caught off guard, Larissa answered, "I--uh—well, I hadn't really thought about it. I'm sort of new at praying." She paused, rubbed her right temple in thought, then nodded. "Okay, I think I've got something." They bowed their heads again, then Larissa began. "Lord, you never heard from me before I met Derrick, but I promise I won't be a stranger from now on. He led me to you . . . and there's nothing better that a man can do for someone." She sniffled, then added, "Lord, Derrick joked with me even in his dying days that he wanted to spend eternity in the southern part of heaven where people talk like he does. I don't know if he made reservations, but I'm sure you'll take good care of him . . . I miss him . . . I always will. Amen."

Passing the urn back to Larissa, Karen said, "Derrick would want you to do it, I'm sure."

The wind again blew Karen's hair into her face; Larissa's was too short to fall into hers. Scattered snowflakes drifted around the two, an occasional one resting on their shoulders. Stooping to her knees and lifting the lid of the urn, Larissa tilted it to its side, its contents sprinkling into a more calm wind, lightly dusting the surface of the water, then gradually disappearing below, all physical evidence of Derrick's existence now gone.

Looking up at the sky, Larissa whispered, "Rest high."

Karen leaned over to help Larissa regain her footing on the shifting floating pier, sniffling and wiping her eyes. "That was . . . absolutely beautiful," she said. The two embraced and shared a final cry over their loss. As they started back down the pier toward the house, Larissa paused. In a moment of clarity, she looked back up at the house and became flooded with emotion. Like Karen, she could almost feel Derrick beside her, waiting to go back to the living room to light a fire and sit on the sofa together.

Hurrying along the length of the pier back to solid ground to escape the cold, Larissa said, "Karen, I've made my decision."

"And?"

"I want you to own the house. But do you mind if I stay here for a while? Maybe it'll be even longer than I'm thinking, but I want this place to be yours. Maybe Derrick really wasn't in his right mind, but I do think he would want me to live here for a while."

"That's wonderful!" Karen said as they walked up the gentle slope back to the house. "And I'll still be praying that you'll change your mind and decide to stay forever."

Larissa laughed. "You and Derrick were cut from the same cloth. You're both wonderful people."

Nearing the house, they stepped onto the deck. "You can stay till the cows come home if you want to," Karen said. "I mean it. Years and years, it's fine with me."

For the first time it dawned on Larissa how difficult it would be to leave this place. She hadn't realized how connected she had become to it.

On the deck, the puppy raced up to Larissa and yipped happily at her feet, hopping around and whining, inviting her to play. She picked him up and stroked the short fur of his back as she hugged the dog against her chest. A sentimental charge raced through Larissa as she held the dog out toward Karen. "Karen," she said, "I'd like to introduce you to Scooter."

END

Afterword

Thank you for purchasing and reading this novel.

Innocence Denied was written with unbelievers in mind, but therein lies a problem—unbelievers would never choose to read a Christian novel.

I'm asking for your help in getting this book into the hands of those who could benefit from it most. My hope is that unbelievers may get hooked into the story and characters first, then be more receptive to the Christian theme that later follows between Derrick and Larissa.

Please join me in this mission by giving this book to someone whom you know to be a doubter or unbeliever. Challenge this person to read the first two chapters.

You and I, together, can make a major impact on someone's life.

Thank you for joining me in this unorthodox manner to bring lost souls closer to our Lord and Savior.

God bless us all,

Mike Garrett